ALIAS™

THE

SERIES

THE ROAD NOT TAKEN

Taking a deep breath to steady her nerves, Sydney climbed over the guardrail and set her feet down on the outer edge of the tiny platform. There was only an inch or two of metal to stand on, so she held on to the rail with both hands as she peered around the side of the speeding express train in search of the local train up ahead. The empty local track ran parallel to the express track, on the inside lane. Iron columns, spaced at regular intervals, rose between the two sets of tracks. Sydney had to be careful not to lean out too far. Her skull would not survive even a glancing collision with one of the sturdy metal girders.

The 4 train zipped past the 51st Street station without stopping. The 6 train had a head start on her, but the 4 was faster. To her relief, she spied the taillights of the 6. Just as she had hoped, the express train was catching up with the local.

Sydney's muscles tensed in preparation. She was only going to get one chance at this, and the timing was going to be a matter of life and death. She was going to have to jump between the iron girders at the exact moment that the two trains were running side by side, when the rear platforms on both trains were right across from each other. One wrong move, and she would end up smashed into a pillar or electrocuted by the tracks.

At least if I screw up, I won't live long enough to regret it, she thought morbidly.

Also available from

SIMON SPOTLIGHT ENTERTAINMENT

ALIAS™

TWO OF A KIND?

FAINA

COLLATERAL DAMAGE

REPLACED

ALIAS™

THE

SERIES

THE ROAD NOT TAKEN

BY GREG COX

An original novel based on the
hit TV series created by J. J. Abrams

SSE

SIMON SPOTLIGHT ENTERTAINMENT

New York London Toronto Sydney

This book is a work of fiction. Any references to historical events, real people, or real locales are used fictitiously. Other names, characters, places, and incidents are the product of the author's imagination, and any resemblance to actual events or locales or persons, living or dead, is entirely coincidental.

SSE

SIMON SPOTLIGHT ENTERTAINMENT
An imprint of Simon & Schuster
1230 Avenue of the Americas, New York, New York 10020

Manufactured in the United States of America
First Edition 10 9 8 7 6 5 4 3 2 1
Library of Congress Control Number 2005925288
ISBN-13: 978-1-4169-0248-5
ISBN-10: 1-4169-0248-1

ACKNOWLEDGMENTS

My second assignment for APO went just as smoothly as the first, thanks to the dedicated efforts of my fellow agents. This debriefing would not be complete unless I thanked the cast and creators of the *Alias* television series for giving me so much to work with; my editors, Patrick Price and Emily Westlake, for their support and advice; my agents, Russell Galen and Ann Behar, for handling the business end of things; and author Jim Young for advice on matters diplomatic. (Any errors or fabrications are, of course, my own.)

Finally, I could not have completed this mission successfully without my family of home-front operatives: Karen, Alex, Churchill, Henry, and Sophie.

INTELLIGENCE BRIEFING

To: Authorized Personnel Only
From: Archives (Classified)
Re: Mission Chronology

Note: the events described in this dossier take place shortly before APO Mission 4.14, codenamed "Nightingale."

PROLOGUE

A CALIFORNIA SUBURB
TWENTY-FIVE YEARS AGO

"What are you doing, Mommy?"

Six-year-old Sydney Bristow watched her mother sitting across the kitchen table, reading through a stack of papers. Occasionally, her mom scribbled on the papers with a bright red pencil. Yellow cupboards and tile gave the kitchen a warm, sunny feel.

"Just grading some English assignments, honey." Laura Bristow looked up from the papers and smiled at her daughter. She brushed her long, dark hair back behind her ear. Sydney looked on admiringly, hoping that someday she would be just as beautiful as her mommy. "What's the matter? Bored?"

"A little," Sydney admitted. Cartoons blared from the living room, but she had seen them before. Daddy was away on business, as usual. Sydney knew he had a Very Important Job, but sometimes she wished he were home more. Clutching her favorite stuffed koala, she clambered up onto the chair next to her mom's. She tried to read the papers too, but there were too many big words for her. "How do you know what grades to give them?"

"That depends," her mother said. She scribbled a "B-" on the top paper, then drew a red circle around it. "I grade on lots of things: spelling, grammar, punctuation, originality. Plus, most important, the ability to communicate." She gave Sydney a serious look. "Always remember, honey. If you know how to express yourself the right way, you can convince anyone of *anything*."

Sydney nodded solemnly, holding her koala on her lap. "That's why it's so important to learn English and other languages, right?" She was already getting lessons on how to speak Spanish, and was supposed to be starting on French soon.

"And why you wanted to be a teacher?"

"Naturally," her mother assured her. "I can't imagine anything more rewarding."

Sydney was impressed. Mommy's job sounded much more important than selling airplane parts like Daddy, even if Daddy had to fly all over the world for his job. "When I grow up," she declared, "I want to be just like you!"

A funny sort of smile appeared on her mother's face. "Maybe you will be."

Three days later, "Laura Bristow" died in a car crash.

CHAPTER 1

LONDON, ENGLAND
NOW

A frozen dragon presided over the celebration.

The imposing ice sculpture, chiseled into the likeness of a rampant Chinese dragon, rested atop a table in the center of the room. More than three feet tall, it towered over the punch bowl, while serving as the centerpiece for a lavish publication party being thrown by one of the U.K.'s leading publishing houses. Throngs of authors, agents, publicists, reviewers, columnists, and other invited guests crowded the second floor of a venerable bookshop on Charing Cross Road. Liveried servers wove among the milling guests, bearing trays of hors d'oeuvres. Oversize cardboard blow-ups of an ornate book jacket were mounted on easels in various corners of the room. *Inside the Dragon: My Years in the Chinese Secret Police* read the title on the cover. Smaller type identified the author as simply "Citizen Ghost."

According to advance hype, the potential best-seller offered the inside scoop on the Red Chinese intelligence apparatus, much to the dismay of Beijing, which had vehemently protested its publication. For better or for worse, however, Her Majesty's government had been in no position to block the publication of the anonymous tell-all. To no one's surprise, the Chinese ambassador had declined to attend the party.

Security was tight, but that hadn't stopped Sydney from attending the exclusive bash. A curly platinum blond wig concealed her natural brown tresses, while a blue chiffon cocktail dress showed off her athletic figure. A silvery metallic sash, which had given the metal detectors downstairs conniptions, was belted around her waist, adding a feminine, sexy touch. Sydney lingered by the refreshments table, sipping from a wineglass as she scoped out the scene.

Rumor had it that a contract had been placed on Citizen Ghost's life, as a warning to others who might consider spilling classified state secrets. Sydney's assignment was to keep the anonymous author alive, as his assassination would place a severe strain on relations between mainland China and the West. Both the British and U.S. governments were reluctant to take a visible role in the dispute between Ghost and his former employers for fear of heightening an already tense situation, so it had fallen upon APO—a covert black ops division of the CIA—to provide Ghost with an extra degree of officially unsanctioned protection.

Let's hope he doesn't need it, Sydney thought. If she was lucky, all she would have to do tonight was sample the canapés and keep a discreet eye on the guest of honor. *Sounds good to me.* She could use an easy mission after all she'd been through lately. Between getting buried alive in Cuba last week and the daily tension at APO, a boring stint of bodyguard duty sounded like a tropical vacation.

At the moment, Citizen Ghost was signing books at a table at the other end of the room. An Oriental dragon mask covered the upper half of his face, concealing his identity and contrasting sharply with his Western-style tuxedo. Stacks of hardcovers were piled on the tablecloth in front of him, and at least a dozen guests waited in line for an autographed first edition. Sydney noted that he signed the books with his left hand, perhaps to disguise his handwriting, and wore latex gloves to avoid leaving any telltale fingerprints on the books. She wondered briefly whether Ghost had actually written his memoir, or if he had been assisted by some obscure ghostwriter.

How ironic would that be?

A pair of burly bodyguards loomed behind the nameless author, but Sydney was unimpressed by the security provided by Ghost's publishers. The two men looked like glorified rent-a-cops, mostly there for show. Ditto for the attractive young Asian woman serving as Ghost's official "taster." She made a big production of sampling Ghost's drinks and hors d'oeuvres before he consumed them, but Syd knew that this would hardly stop a first-class assassin from poisoning Ghost with a sufficiently slow-moving toxin. If someone really wanted the whistle blower dead, they wouldn't mind killing off a publicist or two to get to him. She was more appreciative of the heavy drapes that had been drawn over the bookstore's second-floor windows to discourage snipers. That made her job a little easier; the sheer number of warm bodies crammed into the party rendered infrared gun sights virtually useless.

Time to check in with the guys. Lifting her glass to her lips, Sydney subvocalized into her concealed comm. "Phoenix to Outrigger. Any unpleasant surprises coming my way?"

"Negative, Phoenix," Dixon's voice whispered into her ear. He and Vaughn were stationed outside the bookshop, watching the entrances for late arrivals. "No hostiles on the guest list so far."

"Glad to hear it. Shotgun?" she prompted.

"Likewise," Michael Vaughn reported. Her boyfriend's voice brought a smile to her lips as she imagined his lean, handsome features. "Nobody slipping in the back way."

"Roger," she confirmed. "Ghost watch in progress. Phoenix out."

So far, so good, she thought, cutting off the transmission. *Maybe this will turn out to be a false alarm after all.*

"'Scuse me, luv." A slightly tipsy-looking gentleman stepped in front of her, blocking her view of Citizen Ghost. His ruddy complexion suggested that he had hit a pub on his way to the party. "Care for a refill on your drink?"

"Why, thank you!" Sydney chirped, not bothering to disguise her American accent. London was full of bright young women from the States. She shifted position to get Ghost back in sight, and offered the other guest her glass. He ladled some fresh punch into the goblet, sloshing a bit over the sides. "I can't believe how warm it is in here, even with the air conditioning."

"That's publishing for you. All hot air." He returned Sydney's drink to her and introduced himself. "Nigel Barnett. I'm an agent."

So am I, Syd thought, *although not of the literary variety.* "Marci Plummer."

"Pleased to meet you, Marci." He seemed intent on chatting her up. "So what do you do for a living?"

She flashed him a mischievous grin. "You're looking at it. I'm what they call a 'party motivator.' I'm basically professional eye candy hired to add a touch of glamour to the proceedings." Sydney had been surprised to discover, in *USA Today* of all places, that struggling models and actresses were sometimes paid to attend parties, but she had instantly recognized what a convenient cover story it would make while infiltrating ritzy soirees like this one. "Some of the other girls here are working for a paycheck too."

Sydney regretted that Nadia wasn't among the women she was referring to. The extra backup would have been nice, but her half sister was still finishing up an assignment in Belize. What with the war on terror, APO kept them both pretty busy these days.

"Well, God bless you and your fellow motivators!" Nigel enthused, checking out another suspiciously attractive partyer. "I can just imagine how dreary these affairs would be with nothing but writers and reviewers in attendance." He feigned a shudder at the thought. "I'm sure you're worth every pence."

"Thanks." *I think,* she added silently to herself. She hoped the agent wasn't getting the wrong idea about her assumed profession. Keeping one eye on Citizen Ghost, she scanned the line of people waiting for his autograph. *Quite a turnout.* She fantasized about writing her own memoirs, if and when she ever retired from the spy trade. *On second thought,* she decided after a moment's reflection, *nobody would ever believe it.*

A face caught her eye and a jolt of adrenaline shot through her veins. The face, which belonged to one of the ubiquitous servers, bore a distinct resemblance to that of Niccolo Genovese, a notorious paid assassin. Sydney had never encountered Genovese before, but she had reviewed his dossier as part of her routine training at APO, and his physical similarity to the server was too close for comfort. She watched with apprehension as the server, bearing a carafe of fresh ice water, wound his way through the crowd toward Citizen Ghost.

But was it really Genovese? It was hard to tell. The spiky blond hair was wrong—Genovese was supposed to be a redhead—but Sydney knew how little that meant; she wasn't exactly looking like herself at the moment. Still, it had been months since she had last perused the assassin's file, and the grainy surveillance photos had hardly been museum quality. Plus, there were way too many bad guys out there, and their faces started to blur together after a while. *I need to be certain,* she realized. *A man's life is at stake.*

"Excuse me," she said abruptly, stepping away from a disappointed Nigel. "I just remembered an important phone call I have to make." She retrieved her cell phone from her purse and quickly snapped a photo of the spiky-haired server. *Thank goodness for modern communications technology,* she thought. Now that everyone and his brother had a camera phone, there had been no need to smuggle a hidden spy camera past the guards downstairs.

"Phoenix to Merlin," Sydney whispered, paging Marshall back at APO headquarters in Los Angeles. "Prepare for photo uplink." She transmitted the photo over to Marshall, who had immediate access to the best facial-recognition software on the planet. "I need a positive ID on Niccolo Genovese . . . ASAP."

"Got it, Phoenix," Marshall answered from eight time zones away. Sydney could visualize the diminutive op-tech guy in his office back at the bunker, surrounded by banks of sophisticated electronic equipment. Even as they spoke, a computer was rapidly comparing the snapshot of the server to all known photos of Genovese. She held her breath while tracking the hopefully soon-to-be-identified server with her eyes. "Bingo, Phoenix," Marshall reported within seconds. "We have an 89.9 percent match. He's your guy." There was a momentary pause, during which time he had obviously scanned Genovese's record. "Whoa! Watch yourself, Phoenix. This guy sounds like bad news."

"Roger that, Merlin," Sydney said grimly. She dropped her cell phone back into her purse.

Across the crowded room, Genovese approached the table where Citizen Ghost was still signing books for his prospective readers. The disguised assassin refilled the author's glass, and the highly photogenic taster obligingly lifted the glass toward her lips. . . .

"No!" Sydney shouted, breaking her cover. She had no idea who the taster was or what she really did for a living, but she wasn't about to let the young woman sip from the poisoned goblet. She wanted to rush forward and dash the glass from the woman's hand, but there were too many people in the way. "Don't drink that!"

The taster blinked in confusion. Syd couldn't tell if the other woman was getting the message or not. The edge of the goblet was poised dangerously at the taster's lips.

Taking no chances, Sydney snapped the stem of her own wineglass in half, then hurled the base of the glass like a throwing star. The improvised missile spun through the air, narrowly missing the heads and shoulders of the intervening guests, before smashing into the glass in the taster's hand. The goblet shattered in an explosion of broken glass and ice. Tainted water splattered the woman's dress and soaked the tablecloth before her. She let out a startled yelp. Citizen Ghost leaped to his feet in alarm, while his bodyguards stared balefully at Sydney.

You're looking the wrong way, she thought impatiently. "The server!" She pointed an accusing finger at the spiky-haired killer. Genovese glared murderously at Sydney. "He's an assassin!" She repeated the warning in Mandarin, just in case Ghost didn't speak English. *"Xiong shou!"*

Confused, the guards hesitated, looking back and forth between Sydney and Genovese. The other guests, including her former admirer, Nigel, pulled away from the platinum-blond stunner as though she had the plague. One of the guards reached underneath his jacket for his gun. "Don't move, either of you!" he barked.

But Genovese was too fast for him. Spotting another server nearby, the resourceful hit man snatched a pair of steaming shish kebabs from the other man's tray. "Watch ou—" Sydney began, yet before she could even complete the warning,

Genovese flung the metal skewer like a harpoon, stabbing the bodyguard in the heart. The man's meaty face barely registered his surprise before he toppled backward, crashing against the draped window behind him. The plate glass fragmented beneath his weight and he tumbled through the broken window to the street two stories below. The sound of his heavy body hitting the pavement was immediately followed by shrieks from outside.

Pandemonium erupted within the bookshop as well. Screams and curses echoed off the walls of the densely packed party, adding to the clamor from the sidewalk below. Abandoning any vestige of British reserve, the frantic men and women scrambled for the exits, kicking and clawing at one another in their desperate attempts to get away from the chaos. White-faced and shaking, the young Asian taster dived under the table. *Smart girl,* Sydney thought. Plates and glasses hit the hardwood floor as the other servers joined the frightened guests in their panicky exodus. Sydney wished they were all safely outside already. This was no longer a place for civilians.

"Phoenix to backup!" she alerted Vaughn, Dixon, and headquarters. "We have a situation!"

Hoisting the second shish kebab like a spear, Genovese tried to get a good shot at Citizen Ghost, but there were too many fleeing bodies in the way. The remaining guard stepped between Ghost and the frustrated assassin. The big man drew his gun but appeared reluctant to fire into the chaotic mob. He cast an uncertain glance at Sydney.

"Get him out of here!" she shouted. Ignoring the distraught people rushing past her, she threw the rest of her wineglass at Genovese to get his attention. He ducked his head just in time to avoid the missile. "What's the matter, Niccolo?" she taunted him. "Finding it hard to kill a Ghost?"

The assassin's expression darkened at the mention of his name. *"Puttana!"* he cursed. A heavy Italian accent further confirmed his identity.

"This way! Hurry!" the bodyguard instructed Citizen Ghost as he hustled the author toward the nearest stairway, using his bulk and brandished firearm to clear a path through the fleeing guests. The gun-wielding guard looked more than willing to let Sydney handle Genovese. She let out a sigh of relief as the bodyguard disappeared down the stairs with his charge.

Now it was just her and the cornered assassin.

She knew Sloane and her father would want her to apprehend Genovese for interrogation. *I need to take him alive, if possible.*

The bogus server had more lethal intentions. Raising the skewer above his head like a dagger, he charged at Sydney across the emptying room. “Bitch!” he snarled. “I’ll teach you to interfere with my business!”

Thanks to the tight security, Sydney was unarmed. Looking about quickly for something with which to defend herself, she spotted a discarded aluminum serving tray lying on one corner of the punch table. She snatched up the shiny metal disk with both hands, converting it into a shield. The sharpened point of the skewer scraped against the underside of the tray as she deflected Genovese’s blow.

By now they had the second floor pretty much to themselves. Syd knew that Vaughn and Dixon had to be on their way. Even without her open comm, they couldn’t have missed the first body-guard taking a nosedive out the window. *I just need to keep Genovese here until the guys can shove their way past the guards downstairs and the crowd rushing in the opposite direction . . . unless*

Niccolo has reinforcements too. Wasn't there something in his file about a partner?

Genovese didn't give her a chance to search her memory. Renewing his attack, he stabbed at her again and again, forcing her to parry with the shield. The repeated blows dimpled the shallow bottom of the tray as the iron spit threatened to pierce the sturdy aluminum. The force of the jabs vibrated down Sydney's arms, and she was driven backward by the relentless assault. She kicked out at the assassin's legs, but he deftly evaded her strikes, taking advantage of the extra reach the foot-long skewer gave him.

"Who are you?" he demanded harshly. "Who are you working for?"

"The Writers Guild?" Sydney quipped.

The skewer came at her again, and she stepped backward to brace herself for the blow. To her dismay, however, her high heels came down in a puddle of spilled ice and punch, and she lost her balance. Her legs slid out from beneath her and she landed flat on her back upon the floor, hitting the wooden planks hard enough to knock the breath out of her. Cold punch soaked through the back of her chiffon dress.

Great.

Seizing the opportunity, Genovese lunged at her with the skewer. Sydney had managed to hold on to the tray during her fall, though, and she held it up in front of her. The tray blocked the jab again, but the point of the spit punched through the aluminum at last, coming to rest only a few inches from her face. Keeping to the side, in order to avoid Sydney's futile kicks, Genovese shifted his weight to press down harder against the punctured shield. Sydney realized she was only seconds away from having the shish kebab driven through her skull.

Like hell! she thought. She jerked the circular tray suddenly to the left, wrenching the trapped skewer from Genovese's grip. Before he could grab on to it again, she tossed both tray and skewer away from them as hard as she could. They clattered to the floor on the other side of the room.

"*Donnaccia!* I'll kill you with my bare hands!" Powerful fists seized her throat, throttling her. Sydney reached out desperately and her fingers wrapped around the wooden leg of one of the easels displaying the giant-size blowups of *Inside the Dragon*'s front jacket. She tugged on the flimsy wooden support and both easel and artwork came crashing down on Genovese's head and shoulders.

The distraction loosened the assassin's grip enough for Sydney to break free and roll away. Putting several feet between herself and Genovese, she sprang to her feet, kicking off her stiletto heels before they could betray her again. *So much for high fashion.* As far as she was concerned, the glam part of her assignment was over.

Genovese angrily knocked the fallen easel aside. Moving quickly, while Sydney was still regaining her footing, he ran to retrieve another shish kebab from the floor. Obviously, hehadn't managed to smuggle a gun into the party either.

Sydney glanced briefly at the broken window; unfortunately the first guard had taken his pistol with him when he fell through the glass. Improvising, she undid the metallic sash around her waist and cracked it like a whip. Genovese closed on her cautiously, skewer in hand, and she lashed out with the sash. The metallic fabric grabbed on to the skewer and she yanked it from the killer's hand. Sydney snapped her wrist and the captured spit went flying across the room.

"Give it up, Niccolo!" she urged him. She cracked her sash for emphasis, flaunting the hard steel buckle at the end of the whip. She moved between Genovese and the stairs. "You're not going anywhere except into custody."

"Never!" he growled back at her. Retreating back toward the autographing table, he took hold of one of the heavy hardcovers and pitched it at Sydney's head. "Have a book on me!"

Sydney ducked, but the hefty tome clipped her on the shoulder. *Ouch!* she thought, wishing Citizen Ghost (or citizen ghostwriter) had been less verbose. Wincing, she jumped backward before the book could land on her bare feet. Her shoulder felt numb, but she tightened her grip on the sash to keep from dropping it.

Genovese grabbed another book off the pile and hurled it at Sydney. He bolted for the stairs, circling around the center table to avoid the female agent. Escape, it seemed, had replaced killing Sydney as his first priority.

Forget it! she thought, dodging the second hardcover. She waited until the huge ice dragon was directly between her and the fleeing assassin, then slammed her shoulder into the frozen sculpture. Roughly four hundred pounds of chiseled ice crashed down on top of Genovese, knocking him to the floor. The dragon shattered into pieces.

Genovese moaned pitifully from beneath a heap of cold, translucent shards.

I guess shouting "Freeze!" would be redundant, Sydney thought.

She raced around the table to reach the downed killer. He looked stunned, but she kept up her guard, just in case he was playing possum. Footsteps sounded upon the stairs and a familiar voice called out. "Phoenix!" Vaughn shouted, too well-trained to use her real name in public. "Are you all right?"

"I'm fine!" She felt a rush of relief as Vaughn and Dixon burst into the room, guns in hand. If they hurried, they could still get the assassin out of there before the local authorities arrived to complicate matters. "I have Genovese."

"That's what you think, bitch!" he snapped. Before Sydney could stop him, Genovese plucked an icy talon from the wreckage around him and raked it across his throat, slicing through his right carotid artery. Bright arterial blood gushed from his neck, turning the splintered remains of the sculpture into a mass of gory slush.

No! Sydney thought, caught off guard by Genovese's lethal attack on himself. The Italian hit man was supposed to be a cold-blooded contract killer, not a political or religious fanatic. She had never expected him to take his own life. She considered trying to save him, but there was no point. At the rate he was bleeding, he would be dead in seconds. *I don't understand. Why did he do this?* She stared into his glazed eyes. "Why?"

But the dying assassin was already beyond answering her.

"We should leave," Dixon advised sternly. A worried expression deepened the lines on his severe features. Sirens sounded in the streets outside, drawing closer to the bookshop. "There's nothing more we can do here."

"Just a second," Sydney said. She knew Dixon was right to be concerned, but there was still one thing left to do. Brushing aside the bloody ice, she searched the pockets of Genovese's server's uniform. Her fingers closed on the slim, metallic contours of a compact cell phone. Perhaps the phone contained some intel of interest to APO? She confiscated it and rose to her feet. "Okay," she said to the other two agents. "Let's go."

As Vaughn and Dixon escorted her toward the stairs, she glanced back over her shoulder at the mess she and Genovese had left behind, including the assassin's own bloodless body. A terrified face peeked out from beneath the autographing table and Sydney remembered the hapless taster whose life she had saved. The memory of that accomplishment went a long way toward overcoming her shock and disappointment at failing to take Genovese alive. *If not for me, both that woman and Citizen Ghost might well be dead by now.*

I can live with that.

"Wait!" the perplexed young woman called out. "Who the hell are you people?"

"Just a bunch of party crashers," Syd answered.

CHAPTER 2

APO BUNKER
LOS ANGELES

If one had been escorted blindfolded to the top-secret headquarters of APO, or "Authorized Personnel Only," and then had the blindfold abruptly removed, one would never have guessed that the sleek, high-tech nerve center was actually located in an abandoned bomb shelter beneath the Los Angeles subway system. White steel walls and frosted glass panels gave the subterranean installation a cold, antiseptic appearance, livened up only by the red leather upholstery on the office furniture. A minimal staff toiled in the cubicles outside the main operations areas, all without the "official" sanction of the Central Intelligence Agency. As far as the world was concerned, APO did not exist.

"You're to be commended for your efforts in London," Arvin Sloane addressed the senior agents under his command, who were gathered in the briefing room adjacent to his office. Despite his slight physique and unimposing stature, he gave off an almost palpable aura of authority and even menace. His shrewd eyes peered out through the wire-frame glasses resting on the bridge of his nose, and a thin white beard frosted his jaw. His stylish black suit was impeccably tailored. "Citizen Ghost, aka Song Wei Ling, formerly of the Chinese secret service, remains alive and well and is currently enjoying the number one slot on the *London Times* bestseller list. Although there has been much speculation in the press regarding the incident at the publication party, none has been directed toward us. Director Chase continues to deny any CIA involvement in the affair." Sloane nodded at Sydney, who was seated at the briefing table with her fellow agents. "Well done, Sydney."

Sloane's praise failed to elicit a smile from the female operative. Although she had reluctantly come to terms with Arvin Sloane's role in APO, she could never forget what kind of man he really was. Sloane had betrayed nearly everyone at the table at one time or another, and had personally ordered the deaths of both Sydney's fiancé and her oldest friend. She neither sought nor relished his approval. "Thank you," she said coolly. "What about Genovese? Did we learn anything useful from his cell phone?"

"You bet!" Marshall Flinkman enthused from the other side of the table. Short and fidgety, he sometimes reminded Sydney of an unusually brainy Munchkin. "Your boy, Niccolo, thought he had erased any incriminating data, but he underestimated the sort of high-tech wizardry some of us are capable of." He took a little bow. "It required a bit of tweaking, but I finally managed to retrieve pretty much his entire personal phone directory. Boy, I wouldn't want his wireless bill. Who knew contract killers were in such demand?"

"One listing is particularly worrisome," Sloane announced, cutting off Marshall's characteristic digression. "It belongs to the New York office of the Mexican ambassador to the United Nations."

Sydney didn't like the sound of that. Who at the

Mexican Consulate had been dealing with a well-known professional assassin? She had to assume that the calls had not been social in nature, so who was to have been Genovese's next target?

"What do we know about the Mexican Consulate in New York?" Jack Bristow asked. Sydney's father sat across from her, wearing a conservative gray suit. His stiff, neutral expression was as inscrutable as ever, but Sydney accepted that as simply part of who he was. Although their relationship had gone through a rough spell earlier this year after she learned the truth about her mother's death—Sydney shuddered at the image of her father shooting her mother—they had started to become more comfortable with each other again.

In response to Jack's query, Sloane lifted an electronic remote from the table and pointed it at a bank of monitors mounted on the wall. The face of a middle-aged Hispanic male appeared on the screens. He was a distinguished-looking older man, with a full head of silvery hair, neatly combed back from his brow. His bronzed, clean-shaven features gave him the look of ancient Aztec nobility.

"Mexico's current ambassador to the United Nations is Victor Delgado," Sloane explained.

"He's a reformer, risen up from humble origins, with a reputation for integrity and a low tolerance for political corruption."

"That could make him a target," Jack observed cynically.

"Indeed," Sloane concurred. "There's some reason to believe that Delgado received his posting at the United Nations in an attempt by the ruling class to distance him from affairs back home, where his efforts at reform are not always welcome. It's possible that one or more of his political opponents could be looking for a more permanent way to remove him from the picture, hence the involvement of Niccolo Genovese."

"I don't think Delgado has anything more to fear from Genovese," Vaughn, seated to Sydney's left, pointed out. Sydney suspected that his memories of the assassin's gory, self-inflicted demise were just as vivid as her own. "He took himself out of the picture."

"True," Sloane conceded. "But Genovese was hardly the only professional killer available on the market. For all we know, an assassination is still in the works, with someone at the consulate playing a crucial role in the operation."

He let that assessment sink in for a minute. Sydney tried to imagine the international implications of a UN ambassador being assassinated on American soil. She knew the CIA would want them to do everything they could to prevent such a tragedy.

"We should plant an agent in the consulate itself," Marcus Dixon suggested. Having been a CIA director before he returned to the field via APO, he was accustomed to looking at the big picture. "Find out who there was in contact with Genovese."

Sloane smiled slyly. "As it happens, Ambassador Delgado is currently looking for a new tutor for his teenage stepdaughter." He turned toward Syd and she repressed an urge to glare furiously at him in return; like it or not, he was still her boss these days. "Sydney, this strikes me as an ideal opportunity for you to infiltrate the consulate, especially considering your academic background."

She knew what Sloane was referring to. At one time Sydney had pursued a graduate degree in English literature, with an eye toward someday teaching instead of spying. She had even tried to balance her studies with her espionage activities, until the traumatic events of the last few years had driven the final nail into the coffin of her academic career. *Being "dead" for two years will do that,* she thought bitterly.

Would I have made a good teacher, had my life gone in another direction? The question tugged at her heart, raising all sorts of unresolved issues and regrets. Perhaps this mission would help her get back in touch with that part of herself? If nothing else, she had to admit that Sloane's plan made sense.

"I can do that."

"I never doubted it," Sloane said. He passed out folders to Sydney and the other agents. "Dixon, you're going to go undercover as an interpreter at the United Nations to uncover what you can about the consulate in that environment. Vaughn, Weiss, you'll be providing backup for Sydney."

Eric Weiss, Vaughn's best friend from the CIA, grinned at his buddy. The two of them went back a long way. "Big Apple, here we come."

Sydney smiled at his good spirits. She could usually count on the stocky young agent to add a touch of levity to the proceedings.

"What about me?" Nadia Santos asked. Sydney's half sister had recently returned from her mission in Belize. Of mixed Russian and American descent, she had been an agent for the Argentinian Intelligence Service before being recruited into APO by her father, Arvin Sloane. Her dark hair and sultry good looks complemented her sister's, and often allowed her to pass as Hispanic. "Perhaps I can infiltrate the consulate as well?"

Sloane shook his head. "I want you and Jack to pursue a separate line of investigation."

Sydney wondered what he had in mind.

CHAPTER 3

MEXICAN CONSULATE
MANHATTAN

The consul general of Mexico in New York was housed in a six-story brownstone on East 40th Street, about four blocks south of the main United Nations complex on First Avenue. A tricolored Mexican flag with its green, white, and red stripes symbolizing independence, religion, and unity waved above the front entrance. A fringed canvas awning extended out onto the sidewalk in front of the building.

A cold late January wind blew against Sydney as she climbed the steps to the entrance, and she shivered beneath her camel-colored wool peacoat. Thankfully, her present alias did not demand any sort of high-maintenance disguise, so she looked more or less like herself. A pair of square tortoise-shell glasses rested on her nose, below her side-swept brown bangs. Beneath her heavy coat, she wore a blue knit sweater and a conservative gray skirt, more than suitable for a job interview. *Let's hope Ambassador Delgado likes what he sees,* she thought. *At least I'm not dressed up like a belly dancer or dominatrix for a change.*

"Excuse me," she addressed the receptionist as she entered the foyer. "My name is Iris Talbot. I'm here to see the ambassador." A uniformed security guard casually looked her over. The marble floor bore the image of Mexico's national emblem: an eagle posed atop a cactus, eating a snake. Sydney wondered what sort of human serpent might be slithering through the building at this very second. "I believe I'm expected."

The receptionist took her coat and buzzed someone on the intercom. "The deputy consul will be with you shortly," she informed Syd.

She didn't have to wait long. Within minutes a well-dressed man in his mid-thirties descended the grand staircase leading to the upper stories of the brownstone. Having thoroughly researched the consulate and its staff, she recognized him as Manuel Rivera, the ambassador's right-hand man, but let him introduce himself anyway.

"A pleasure to meet you, Ms. Talbot," he said, taking her hand. His eyes widened in appreciation of Sydney's good looks, and he held on to her hand a second too long. She caught a whiff of expensive cologne. "I must say, I wish my old tutors had been as attractive as you. I probably would have paid more attention in class." His impeccable grooming and suave, slightly calculating manner reminded her unpleasantly of her former adversary Julian Sark, but she resolved not to hold that against him. "The ambassador will see you now. Please follow me."

He escorted her up the stairs to Delgado's office, which was located on the third floor of the brownstone. The office door was wide open, suggesting that the consulate staff might occasionally have access to the ambassador's office—and private phone. A pair of masculine voices escaped the office as they approached. Sydney pretended not to eavesdrop.

"The opera is expected to let out around ten thirty P.M.," a gruff voice announced. "A limo will be waiting, and Ramon will accompany Senora Delgado to see that she arrives home safely."

Sydney and Rivera lingered in the doorway while Ambassador Delgado conferred with another man, whom Sydney recognized as Carlos Allende, the consulate's chief of security. A heavyset man with a stiff, military demeanor, Allende stood before Delgado's desk while the ambassador inspected some paperwork. His hands were clasped behind his back, like the commandant in an old World War II flick.

"Bueno." Delgado chuckled to himself as he handed the approved itinerary back to Allende. "I'm tempted to offer Ramon my condolences. I've always found operas to be tedious in the extreme."

"A bodyguard's duty involves many sacrifices," Allende said drily.

Rivera cleared his throat, and the two men noticed him and Sydney standing in the doorway. "Ah, our prospective new tutor!" Delgado said expansively. He rose from his seat behind the desk and beckoned to them. "Please come in!"

The ambassador was even more charismatic in

person than in the photos and news clips Sydney had studied in preparation for her mission. He was trim and fit for a man his age, and his handshake was firm and welcoming. Warmth and congeniality radiated from his sparkling brown eyes and ready smile. Sydney found it hard to believe that a member of his own staff might want him dead, if the ambassador was indeed the target of an assassination plot. *Careful,* she reminded herself. *Let's not make any rash assumptions.* Who knew whom Genovese was supposed to murder?

"Buenos días, Señor Embajador," she greeted him.

Delgado reacted with delight. "Your Spanish is *muy excelente.*"

"As is your English," she replied sincerely.

Allende started to leave, but Delgado insisted on introducing him first. "Senor Allende is responsible for ensuring the safety of myself and my family," he explained, "as well as the general security of the consulate."

"Ms. Talbot," the other man addressed her brusquely. Beneath a bushy black mustache, a permanent scowl seemed impressed on Allende's features. His leathery face was marred by a thin white scar running across his right cheek. A telltale bulge beneath his rumpled jacket informed Sydney that the security chief preferred to be armed on the job. He eyed her dubiously, and she hoped that he was just habitually suspicious of strangers and not distrustful of her in particular. *I'll have to watch myself around him,* she decided, *even if we're both looking out for Delgado's safety.*

Making his apologies, Allende briskly exited the office. "Please be seated," Delgado said to Sydney, gesturing toward one of the wingback chairs facing his large mahogany desk. He waited until she was comfortable before sitting back down himself. Manuel Rivera remained standing, watching over the encounter from a few yards away.

The ambassador's desk was neatly organized, largely free of loose papers and documents. Sydney snuck a peek at the executive speakerphone resting on the desktop. According to Marshall, the number on Genovese's cell phone belonged to the ambassador's private line.

Who else had access to this phone? Rivera? Allende?

Someone else altogether?

She would have to keep a close eye on the

comings and goings in this office, especially when the ambassador was otherwise engaged.

"Thank you for coming in on such short notice," Delgado said. "I'm afraid my stepdaughter's previous tutor suddenly became unavailable."

Sydney knew that was Sloane's doing. A substantial bribe, along with a bit of judicious blackmail, had been sufficient to create the necessary job opening at the Mexican Consulate. Syd just hoped Sloane had employed more carrots than sticks in order to entice the original tutor to take a more lucrative engagement elsewhere.

"No problem," she said. "I've been looking for a position like this for some time. There's nothing like being able to give an individual student plenty of personal attention. The larger the class size, the harder it is to get any actual teaching done."

Delgado nodded approvingly. He removed a cardboard file from his desk and flipped through its contents. "Your résumé and references are quite impressive."

The best APO could manufacture, she thought confidently. Given a couple hours' notice, the crack team back at headquarters could document just about any cover story; Syd knew that her alias would hold up to all but the most intensive scrutiny. "Thank you."

Delgado closed the file, apparently satisfied with what it contained. He leaned forward in his chair and his voice took on a more serious tone. "I have a great respect for teachers." He turned a framed photo toward Sydney. A faded black-and-white snapshot depicted a whitewashed brick building on a dusty city street. A statue of the Virgin Mary resided in a niche above the front doorway, and a handful of nuns posed in front of the structure with a cluster of scruffy-looking children in cheap, hand-me-down clothing.

"I was not always accustomed to such opulent surroundings," he continued, glancing around the elegantly appointed office. "I was raised in a Catholic orphanage in Mexico City. The nuns there were strict, but they imparted to me the importance of education and self-improvement. Thanks to them, I had a chance to make something of myself, instead of ending up dead or in prison like so many other penniless street urchins."

Sydney was impressed by the ambassador's obvious sincerity and depth of feeling. She envied Delgado's stepdaughter, Mercedes. Unlike Sydney, she was apparently not being raised by a distant father and "deceased" mother. "They must be very proud of you."

"You're too kind," he insisted. A flicker of sadness crossed his face. "Alas, I'm afraid those holy sisters have long since gone to their eternal reward." He sighed deeply, then shook off his momentary melancholy. "But enough about me, as you Americans say. You strike me as just the bright and conscientious woman we're looking for to instill a little learning into my stepdaughter's skull." He glanced at Rivera. "Manuel, would you be so kind as to fetch my wife and Mercedes? I would like them to meet the new tutor."

"Of course," the deputy said, and slipped out of the room.

Sydney didn't have to feign her relief that the interview had gone so well.

I'm in, she thought.

Now for the hard part: finding out who here had been in touch with Niccolo Genovese—and why.

"Victor?" An attractive woman strolled into the office. "Manuel said you wanted to see me?"

Catalina Delgado, née Torres, was several years younger than her husband. Her voluptuous figure, which boasted some impressive silicone enhancement, was poured into a cherry red Louis Vuitton dress. Flashy jewelry glittered on her neck, wrists, and fingers. Sydney recalled that Catalina had once been a Mexican movie starlet before trading in her fading film career for the more privileged life of a prominent politician's wife. Her hair, which was dyed a lustrous shade of blond, tumbled onto her shoulders in cascades of golden curls.

"Cariño!" the ambassador welcomed his spouse. "Thank you for coming. I'd like you to meet Mercedes's new tutor, Ms. Iris Talbot."

Sydney rose from her chair to greet the other woman. "Pleased to meet you, Senora Delgado. I'm looking forward to working with your daughter."

"Please, call me Catalina," she insisted, taking Sydney's hand. "It will be good to have another woman around this dreary pile of bricks, especially one whose headisn't lost in politics all the time." Letting go of Sydney's hand, she stepped back to inspect the newcomer's outfit. "I love your glasses," she commented after a second. "Gucci?"

"Anne Klein," Syd corrected her.

"*Sí,* of course." Catalina nodded knowingly. "It definitely works for you."

Sydney's thoughts regarding the other woman were somewhat less charitable. *Older man, sexy young wife* . . . It was a scenario right out of a dozen old film noir movies. Was Catalina a gold digger plotting to off her aging husband in favor of a younger model? Just because it was a cliché didn't mean it wasn't a possibility. *I can't rule out Catalina as a suspect.*

"Thanks!" Sydney said perkily. "That's quite a compliment coming from someone of such obvious taste and style."

The ambassador glanced at his watch. "I don't know what's keeping Mercedes," he commented, with a touch of impatience in his voice. Sydney wondered if there was tension between Delgado and his teenage stepdaughter. According to the official records, he and Catalina had only been married for a couple of years.

I wonder how I would have reacted if Dad had remarried after Mom supposedly died, Sydney wondered. In truth, "Laura Bristow" had been an alias of Irina Derevko's, a Russian operative who had faked her death in a car accident. *I'm sure it would have required a bit of an adjustment for all concerned.*

Finally Mercedes arrived on the scene, escorted by Manuel Rivera. Unlike her mother, the thirteen-year-old was casually dressed, in faded jeans and a Marc Anthony T-shirt. A pair of headphones was clamped over her ears, and she bobbed her head in rhythm to a private melody, barely acknowledging the presence of the adults in the room. Her sullen expression gave Sydney the impression that Mercedes was less than enthusiastic about being summoned to her stepfather's office.

Delgado scowled at the girl's behavior. He nodded at Rivera, who blithely plucked the headphones from Mercedes's scalp. Sydney caught a snatch of Latin-flavored hip-hop music before the teenager flicked off her iPod. "Hey, watch it!" she snapped at Rivera. "Keep your hands to yourself."

The ambassador ignored her outburst. "Mercedes," he said firmly, "I'd like you to meet your new tutor, Ms. Talbot. She'll be replacing Ms. Coning, who, as you know, left to take a position elsewhere."

"Yeah, whatever," Mercedes mumbled, demonstrating that she had already mastered American teenspeak. She glanced diffidently at Sydney but did not make eye contact. She slouched in front of her stepfather's desk, her hands dug deep into the front pockets of her jeans. Silver rings and studs pierced her eyebrows, nose, and ears. Green dye streaked her hair. "Is that all? Can I go now?"

"Mercedes, don't be rude!" her mother scolded her. "And straighten up. You look like an old lady with your shoulders hunched like that."

It occurred to Sydney that Catalina must have been incredibly young, no more than a teenager herself, when she had Mercedes. Rumor had it, Mercedes's real father was a now-forgotten Mexican soap star who was no longer in the picture.

"Hey, this was your idea, not mine," the girl shot back. She corrected her posture by a minimal degree. "I wouldn't even need a tutor if you'd just let me stay in my old school like I'd wanted to."

"Mercedes, *cariño,*" Catalina cooed. "I know you miss your little friends back in Mexico, but you must realize what an important opportunity this is for your father."

"Stepfather," Mercedes corrected her pointedly, confirming Sydney's suspicion of strained relations between Victor Delgado and the sulky adolescent. Despite this, she doubted that Mercedes had anything to do with a possible assassination plot.

How on earth would a thirteen-year-old girl get in touch with a highly paid professional killer?

Catalina squirmed in her satin dress, visibly embarrassed by the unpleasant scene playing out in front of the new tutor. *"Lo siento,"* she apologized to Sydney. "Mercedes isn't always like this. It's just that moving to New York, and leaving all her school friends behind, has been very hard on her."

"I understand perfectly," Syd assured her. She offered Mercedes a friendly smile that was conspicuously not reciprocated. Sydney suspected that she had her work cut out for her—not that educating the recalcitrant teenager was her actual objective. "I'm sure Mercedes and I will make the best of the situation."

The girl shrugged in response.

"Excelente," Delgado declared. "How soon can you move in?"

CHAPTER 4

MEXICAN CONSULATE

Sydney's room on the top floor of the consulate was small, but comfortable. Before unpacking, she carefully swept the room for electronic bugs. To her relief, she quickly determined that she was not being monitored. *That makes life easier,* she thought. At least she didn't have to worry about blowing her cover during a private moment.

Speaking of which, she took out her cell phone and dialed a local number. State-of-the-art encryption software ensured that the line was secure.

"Phoenix to Shotgun," she said, keeping her voice low out of habit. "What's new?"

"Just holding down the fort," Vaughn answered. Although the only window in the room was at the rear of the brownstone, looking out over a small courtyard, she knew that Vaughn and Weiss were ensconced in a third-floor office opposite the consulate, putting them in an ideal location to watch over the front entrance to the building. Sloane had pulled plenty of strings to get them this prime bit of New York real estate, as well as a permanent parking space in front of the building. It gave Syd a sense of relative security to know that she had backup close at hand. "You-know-who is driving me nuts with his card tricks, though."

She grinned at her boyfriend's exasperated tone. Weiss, who was a direct descendant of Harry Houdini, was something of an amateur magician, and always seemed to have some new bit of sleight of hand to show off. Unluckily for Vaughn, he was now a captive audience.

"Think of it as an extended boys' night out," she advised him. It was going to be frustrating, having Vaughn so nearby, yet not being able to be with him. There was no way around it, however; she couldn't take the chance that someone might notice them meeting and get suspicious. As always, the mission took priority over romance. "What have you heard from Dixon?" she asked. The other agent had already started working at the United Nations as an interpreter.

Vaughn's voice grew more businesslike. "He's passed on some interesting intel. Seems Ambassador Delgado is scheduled to address an upcoming special session of the UN on the subject of international drug trafficking. Back home in Mexico, Delgado is known as an ardent foe of the big drug cartels." Syd remembered reading as much in the ambassador's file. "Maybe the drug traffickers intend to kill Delgado before he can testify?"

"Makes sense to me," she agreed. Certainly, the wealthy drug lords were capable of employing the likes of Niccolo Genovese. More so, perhaps, than either Catalina or Mercedes. "We can't discount that scenario."

"In that case, the clock is ticking," Vaughn said. "Delgado is supposed to speak to the UN Commission on Narcotic Drugs on February eighth."

Sydney instantly registered just how urgent her mission had become. If someone indeed intended to kill the ambassador before the special session, then she had barely a week to get to the bottom of the conspiracy.

I'd better get cracking, she realized.

Wasting no time, Sydney finished unpacking and set out to explore the consulate. Although she had memorized the layout of the building from blueprints and floor plans obtained by APO, there was no substitute for firsthand reconnaissance. In her line of work, a thorough knowledge of one's physical environment often meant the difference between life and death. *I hope it won't come to that,* she thought, *but it's best to be ready for anything.*

She quickly reviewed the basic layout in her head.

Sixth floor: servant's quarters, including Sydney's own. Although the consulate employed more than twenty-five people in various capacities, there was only a handful of full-time residents, including the ambassador and his family. Sydney shared the top floor of the brownstone with the valet, the housekeeper, and a couple of maids. The sixth floor was also the site of the small makeshift classroom where she would hold her lessons with Mercedes.

Fifth floor: the Delgados' private apartments, including the master bedroom and bath. Mercedes's room was also on the fifth floor, Sydney recalled from the floor plans. She wondered how often the teenager had friends over, and whether any hostile parties had attempted to infiltrate the building that way.

Fourth floor: devoted to formal dining and entertaining. A small ballroom, complete with a chandelier, was adjacent to both the elegant dining room and the kitchen. As she was merely a paid tutor, Syd doubted that she would be attending any galas.

Third floor: the chief administrative offices. Besides the ambassador himself, both Rivera and Allende had offices here, along with their various aides and secretaries. In theory, the ambassador also maintained an office at the main United Nations complex. Dixon would have to monitor the goings-on there.

Second floor: general office space, where routine consular affairs and the everyday business of the consulate was carried out—visas, passports, baby registrations, reports of death abroad, and other bureaucratic matters. Syd suspected that there was little to be learned there, especially since the researchers back at APO were already scrutinizing the consulate's personnel records for any potential red flags. Last she'd heard, no known terrorists or international assassins had popped up on the consulate's payroll.

First floor: reception. Beyond the impressive foyer, there was also a station for the guards monitoring the entrance, as well as a mail room serving the rest of the consulate.

That left the basement, which reportedly housed a sophisticated electronic communications center. Sydney decided to start at the bottom and work her way up.

Closing the door to her room behind her, she placed a thin piece of transparent plastic across the seam between the door and its frame. The minuscule strip was nearly invisible to the naked eye, but would be silently torn in half if anyone attempted to enter the room in her absence. As far as she knew, she had aroused no suspicions, but if someone did come snooping around, she wanted to know about it. *Standard operating procedure,* she thought. *Better safe than sorry.*

In her hand was what appeared to be a package of miniature Chicklets: tiny pieces of candy-covered gum, each no bigger than a match head. In fact, only the top layer was actually gum. A concealed latch at the bottom of the package allowed her to spill one of the very special "Chicklets" into her palm, one at time. These were miniature listening devices, straight from Marshall's laboratory at APO. Sydney intended to plant a few discreet bugs while she explored the building.

At times like this, she thought, *it's a good thing the CIA keeps its distance from APO.* Bugging foreign consulates was definitely the sort of activity about which the CIA would want to maintain plausible deniability. *If we get caught, we're on our own.*

She popped a piece of real gum into her mouth—for cover purposes—and found the exit leading to the back stairs, which she figured would be less conspicuous. She rapidly descended five flights of stairs, passing a few nameless aides along the way, until she reached the basement door. She tugged the door open and stepped through in a deliberately nonfurtive manner. To her surprise, she was almost immediately confronted by Manuel Rivera.

"Ms. Talbot," he blurted out. "What are you doing down here?"

Syd did not let herself get flustered; she'd been caught in far more incriminating circumstances than these. "Oh, I was just familiarizing myself with the building," she said lightly. "Hope I haven't wandered into anywhere off-limits."

"Not at all," he assured her, shooting her an ingratiating smile. He seemed to welcome the opportunity to get to know the cute new tutor better. "You just need to watch out for that light over there." He pointed to a glowing red bulb mounted above a closed doorway a few yards away. A sign on the door read VIDEO-CONFERENCING CENTER. AUTHORIZED PERSONNEL ONLY.

Sydney tried not to smirk at that last phrase. *Talk about a private joke.* "Video-conferencing?"

"We have a two-way, closed-circuit link to various venues at the United Nations, so that the ambassador can take part in events and conferences even when it is not convenient for him to visit the site in person. At the moment, for example, he's sitting in on a meeting of the Permanent Forum on Indigenous Issues." Rivera stepped closer to Sydney, slightly invading her personal space. "That red light means the ambassador is busy and should not be disturbed. I'm actually waiting to talk to him as soon as the meeting is over."

"How cool," Sydney commented. She immediately appreciated the value of knowing when Ambassador Delgado was otherwise occupied. "The latest in virtual diplomacy, I guess."

"That's one way to put it," Rivera said. He laughed more loudly than her quip deserved, flashing a set of pearly white teeth. He smoothed back his hair, making sure every dark strand was in place. "So tell me, Ms. Talbot, do you have a boyfriend?"

Doesn't waste time, does he? Sydney thought. With his dapper attire and immaculate grooming, the smooth young deputy was probably a hit with the ladies, but she wasn't looking to play Mata Hari on this assignment. Still, she didn't want to discourage him too much. The more he kept trying to flirt with her, the more likely she was to learn about the consulate's inner workings. Getting him to brag about his very important duties here was likely to be a breeze.

"Sorta," she said with an audible lack of conviction. "We're kind of on-and-off."

"And at the moment?" he pressed.

"On." She sighed heavily, glad that Vaughn wasn't monitoring this exchange. "I think. It's complicated, you know?"

"I can imagine," he said sympathetically.

That's what you think. She figured Rivera's head would explode if she actually gave him the full particulars of her rocky relationship with Michael Vaughn. *Like the time I stabbed him in the ribs and left him bleeding in a ditch, just to maintain my cover. Or the time he married a duplicitous double agent who tried to get us both killed.*

"You have no idea," she said.

It occurred to her that with both Delgado and Rivera confined to the basement, now was a good time to bug their offices upstairs. "Anyway, I should probably get going. I need to get some lesson plans ready before tomorrow." She turned back toward the stairs. "Talk to you soon," she promised.

"I can't wait." For a second she was afraid he was going to accompany her up the stairs, but then he remembered the sheaf of papers in his hands and glanced over his shoulder at the video-conferencing room. Apparently, it really was imperative that he speak with the ambassador as soon as possible. "Welcome aboard."

Bypassing the ground floor and the second floor, she went straight to the executive offices on the third floor. It was the middle of a busy weekday afternoon, and the corridors were full of bustling activity. Staff workers hurried about their respective tasks, occasionally nodding at Sydney, or they remained glued to their desks and cubicles. Phones rang, and the hubbub of numerous conversations permeated the air. Someone cursed in Spanish at a temperamental photocopier.

Sydney eased casually toward the ambassador's office. A consulate security pass was clipped to the front of her striped turtleneck sweater.

"Iris!" a cheerful voice greeted her familiarly. She turned to see Catalina Delgado emerge from her office at the end of the corridor. A clearly nonfaux fox stole was draped over the shoulders of her beige paillette coat, and suede stiletto boots carried her down the hall toward Sydney. A beefy young man who resembled a heavyweight boxer followed after her, carrying a pink Fendi handbag that Syd assumed belonged to Catalina. His broad shoulders strained the seams of his black T-shirt and jacket.

"Senora Delgado," Sydney replied.

"Please, I told you, call me Catalina." The ambassador's wife was all smiles. "Are you settling in all right? I know that Mercedes is looking forward to her classes with you."

Sydney didn't need a polygraph test to know that Catalina was bending the truth a bit. "Yes, thank you. My room is very comfortable." She made a mental note to plant a bug in Catalina's office the first chance she got.

"*Muy bien!* Well, I'd love to stop and chat, but I have to run. A luncheon at Tavern on the Green, I'm afraid. Ramon and I were just heading out the door." A thought occurred to her and she paused to introduce her muscular companion. "Have you met Ramon? He's my most dependable bodyguard. I wouldn't think of going anywhere without him."

Is that so? Sydney thought. She instinctively sized the man up as a potential opponent. He had at least six inches and seventy pounds on her, and he looked like he spent a lot of hours at the gym. No obvious signs of steroid abuse, though. He looked younger than Syd, probably in his early twenties. Sydney wondered what, if any, martial arts training he'd received. *I bet I could take him.*

Catalina grabbed on to his arm and tugged him forward. "Ramon, this is Iris Talbot, the new tutor."

"Buenos días," he grunted. He was good-looking, in a thuggish sort of way. A scruffy goatee carpeted his square chin, and his glossy black hair was pulled back into a ponytail. Syd guessed he was the strong, silent type.

"Pleased to meet you," she said.

Catalina glanced at her Rolex. "*Ah mi Dios,* look at the time! Come, Ramon. The car will be waiting." She brushed past Sydney on her way to the front stairs. Ramon lumbered after her, still toting her handbag. Catalina paused at the top of the stairs to blow Sydney a kiss. "*Hasta luego,* Iris!"

Several eyes turned to watch the ambassador's wife depart. Sydney blended into the background while she waited for the staffers to get back to their work. As the daily bustle resumed, no one noticed Sydney slip quietly into the ambassador's office and partly close the door behind her. *That was easy,* she thought. *Too easy.* If she could sneak into the office so effortlessly, who else might be able to do so? Maybe Genovese's would-be employer?

A handwoven Zapotec rug muffled her footsteps, and she smoothly palmed one of her ersatz Chicklets before sticking it unobtrusively onto the underside of Delgado's desk. A special adhesive allowed it to stick to the polished wood but not to Sydney's skin. She stepped away from the desk and looked for another good place to hide a bug, just in case the first one malfunctioned or was discovered. Her father had often impressed on her the importance of redundancy.

A rustic bookcase covered the eastern wall of the office. Besides various books and directories, the shelves also proudly displayed an assortment of citations, awards, and framed photographs of Delgado with such celebrated personages as Salma Hayek and Kofi Annan. The opposite wall was dominated by a large oil painting of a Spanish-style cathedral. Sydney extracted another bug from the bottom of the Chicklets box and approached the portrait. She quickly planted the listening device behind the edge of the gilded wooden frame. Just as she was reaching into her pocket for another bug, she heard a noise behind her. Sydney froze.

"What are you doing here?" a gruff voice challenged her.

Gulping despite herself, Sydney spun around to find Carlos Allende glowering at her. The sour-faced security chief stood between her and the doorway, his fists clenched at his sides. He looked like he was about one second away from calling for a firing squad. "Answer me," he demanded.

"I—I was just looking for the ambassador," she stammered, pretending to be intimidated. She hoped that Allende would not compare notes with Rivera later on. "I couldn't help admiring this painting. It's gorgeous isn't it? Do you know who the artist is?"

Allende snorted dismissively. Apparently he wasn't an art lover. "What's that in your hand?"

"This?" she asked, all innocence. She extracted her hand from her pocket and held out her palm to show him the bite-size morsel, then popped the listening device into her mouth and swallowed. Thankfully, Marshall had designed the bug to pass harmlessly through the human digestive system, although she didn't want to think about what sorts of sounds the miniaturized microphone was likely to pick up over the next several hours. She poured some real gum into her hand.

"Chicklets," she explained. "Want some?"

CHAPTER 5

ROME, ITALY

Coins splashed into the Fontana del Trevi as throngs of tourists carried out the tradition of tossing them over their left shoulders into the fountain. Chiseled from pristine white marble, the triumphant figure of King Neptune posed atop a sculpted shell drawn by winged steeds and a pair of tritons. Female figures swathed in flowing robes occupied smaller niches of their own, separated from Neptune by imposing marble columns. Around two hundred fifty years old, Fontana del Trevi was the largest and most famous fountain in

Rome, completely dominating the cozy piazza in which it dwelt. Crowded steps led down to a basin of clear blue water. As the sunlight faded, floodlights illuminated the baroque marble facade of the fountain. Pastel-colored buildings, painted in shades of red and orange and yellow, struggled to compete for the attention of teeming sightseers. Flower vendors wound through the crowd, hawking fresh roses to passing visitors. Despite the coolness of the evening, the piazza remained packed with tourists. Flashbulbs went off as frequently as the muzzle flares of an automatic weapon.

Jack Bristow sat alone at one of the many sidewalk cafés around the piazza. Opaque sunglasses and a false mustache disguised his identity, not that he imagined he was currently under surveillance. He sipped a glass of wine while sampling a savory bowl of fresh minestrone. Jack lived in a world of constant ambiguity where almost nothing could be taken for granted, but if there was one thing he could be certain of, it was this: It was impossible to get a bad meal in Italy.

He had not come to Rome for the cuisine, however. According to Sloane, Niccolo Genovese was reputed to have had a mysterious silent partner about whom little was known. Indeed, they were known in some circles as "The Fire and The Smoke," with Niccolo, who did most of the actual killing, being The Fire. Jack's assignment was to track down The Smoke in hopes of finding out more about his late partner's dealings with the Mexican consulate in New York City. So far, however, The Smoke had proven just as elusive and hard to grasp as his (or her) namesake.

Had Genovese committed suicide in order to avoid revealing his confederate's name under interrogation? Jack wondered what could inspire such extraordinary loyalty, particularly in a mercenary like Genovese. *A blood relation?* he speculated. Jack knew that he would gladly sacrifice his own life to protect Sydney; indeed, he had already entered into a secret partnership with Arvin Sloane to protect her from her bloodthirsty aunt Elena.

He couldn't help wondering how Sydney was faring in New York. Her current assignment was not as overtly perilous as some, but he understood only too well that every undercover operation held an element of risk. Anyone willing to employ Niccolo Genovese would not hesitate to eliminate an overly inquisitive tutor, especially if her cover was blown. Sydney was playing a dangerous game.

She knows what she's doing, he reminded himself. In any event, he had his own mission to complete. The best way he could protect Sydney right now was to acquire as much intel as possible regarding the Italian assassin connection. The more APO learned about the possible conspiracy, the less Sydney would be navigating in the dark.

"Raptor to Evergreen," he whispered into his comm. "Are you in position?"

Nadia's voice replied in his earpiece. "Affirmative, Raptor. I'm at eleven o'clock."

Jack looked across the piazza. At first he couldn't spot Nadia among the swarm of people admiring the fountain, but then the crowd cleared and he discerned a familiar-looking flower vendor. Nadia wore a low-cut peasant blouse and pleated skirt. Her naturally dark hair tumbled past her shoulders. She clutched a bundle of roses to her chest while holding out a single blossom to the strolling tourists. *"Scusi,"* he heard her plead over the comm-link. "A rose for the beautiful lady?"

She was certainly convincing, Jack acknowledged.

As well she should be. The illegitimate daughter of Arvin Sloane and Irina Derevko, she had deception in her blood.

He instantly regretted the thought. *That was uncharitable.* He had once assured Nadia that he would never blame her for her parents' misdeeds, and he had meant it. Still, Nadia remained a living reminder of his wife's treacherous affair with Sloane, which Jack was never likely to forget. Furthermore, he was acutely aware that, several months ago, he had lied to Nadia about the circumstances of her mother's death, a decision that was likely to have grave consequences should she ever learn that it was he who had actually killed Irina. He winced at the memory of his wife's body sinking to the bottom of that pool in Vienna, a bullet hole in her forehead. *It had to be done,* he reminded himself. *To save Sydney's life.*

There had been no alternative to his pairing with Nadia on this mission, however. Sloane's mission assignments made sense. Jack had the necessary connections in Italy, and Nadia was a logical substitute for Sydney while her sister was engaged elsewhere. In addition, Nadia's prior intelligence activities in Latin America raised the possibility of her being recognized by someone at the Mexican consulate. Better to assign her to Europe instead. Nadia and Jack's tangled personal histories were irrelevant in the context of their larger mission.

We'll just have to make the best of it, he thought.

He compartmentalized his personal misgivings and glanced down at his wristwatch. The target of tonight's operation was likely to be making his appearance any minute now. Jack looked past Nadia to scan the far end of the piazza.

Sure enough, a trio of figures emerged from the doorway of a violet-colored building. Jack recognized the man in the middle as Kao Yun, an expatriate Chinese businessman who was actually the head of the Chinese intelligence's European operations. He was a lanky man wearing a tailored Italian suit. His shaved skull gave him a slightly skeletal look. He was accompanied by three stone-faced Asian bodyguards who probably weighed nine hundred pounds between them. They walked ahead of Kao, clearing a path for their autocratic employer. Jack was aware that Kao had dinner reservations at an exclusive *ristorante* on the Via Stamperia.

Sloane had reason to believe that it was Kao who had hired The Fire and The Smoke to assassinate Citizen Ghost in London. He hoped the Chinese spymaster could point them toward the surviving member of the partnership, provided he could be persuaded to do so.

That was where Nadia came in.

"Raptor to Evergreen," he alerted her. "Target approaching your location. Proceed with operation."

"I hear you loud and clear, Raptor," she answered. "It's showtime."

Kao ignored the yapping tourists infesting the piazza. He'd had a bad day and was looking forward to ordering a large bottle of wine with his dinner. He figured he deserved it after all he had been through lately.

His superiors in Beijing were not happy that Song Wei Ling, alias Citizen Ghost, was still alive, but what was he supposed to do? After that botched assassination attempt in London, Song had gone deep underground to evade further attempts on his life. These days the bestselling traitor made Salman Rushdie look overexposed. *Not that I can blame him,* Kao thought bitterly. *If this keeps up, I may have to go into hiding myself.*

Again his thoughts returned to the identity of the woman who had interfered with the hit. Who had she been working for? MI6? The CIA? Chobetsu? He had managed to obtain footage from the bookshop's security cameras, but the sexy blonde on the tape was unfamiliar to him. *At least Genovese had the decency to kill himself after screwing up the job,* Kao reflected. *That spared me the trouble of having him eliminated.*

Not that Beijing appreciated that silver lining.

"Scusi, signore?" A musical voice intruded upon his gloomy ruminations. He looked up to see a gorgeous young flower peddler approaching him with her arm outstretched. Her slender fingers gripped a solitary rose. Her full red lips glistened moistly. "A flower to brighten your day?"

His bodyguards moved to block the girl's path, but Kao held up his hand. "Wait," he instructed. "Let her through." The lovely vendor was a welcome distraction from his troubles. What could it hurt to give her a few moments of his time? Certainly, it beat arguing on the phone with his impatient superiors.

"Grazie!" she exclaimed. As she slipped past

his guards, he saw that she was even more attractive than he had first realized. The girl's bottomless black eyes entreated him. The cool night air raised goose bumps on her bare arms. "Would the kind gentleman care for a rose?"

"From such a beautiful lady? Why not?" He fished his wallet from his pocket and gave her a handful of euros. She tucked the bills into her bodice, then stepped forward to thread the rose into the lapel of his suit. Smiling, he took advantage of her proximity to sneak a peek at her copious cleavage. The intoxicating fragrance of her perfume filled his nostrils. Maybe wine wasn't all he wanted tonight? "Perhaps you'd care to join me for dinner?" he suggested.

She blushed and backed away. "Perhaps another night?" she said coyly. Before he could protest, she faded back into the crowd surrounding the Fountain of Trevi. Within moments he heard her enthusiastically hawking her overpriced blossoms to a pair of sightseeing Americans. "A flower for the lovely lady? Very romantic!"

Kao sighed and shrugged his shoulders. *Well, it was worth a try,* he mused. At least the shapely flower vendor had somewhat lightened his mood.

He sniffed the rose in his lapel, savoring his memory of the brief but tantalizing encounter. His stomach grumbled and he recalled that his dinner—and the much-anticipated bottle of wine—was waiting. "All right," he addressed his bodyguards, who tactfully refrained from commenting on the girl's swift retreat. "Let's get moving."

Leaving the crowded piazza behind, they turned left past a sidewalk café and strode down a less populated side street. Kao could see the restaurant ahead and wondered what he was in the mood for tonight. Maybe sautéed veal smothered in prosciutto and sage, preceded by a sampling of fresh antipasti. Mouthwatering aromas from the various cafés and restaurants added to his appetite. He could practically taste the antipasti already.

Just then a man stepped in front of Kao and his guards. "Signore Kao?" the man addressed him. He was a fleshy-looking European with a double chin, receding hairline, and pencil-thin mustache. "Enrico Albani, National Security." He flashed a badge in front of Kao and the other men. "I need a moment of your time."

Kao's bodyguards tensed in readiness but wisely

refrained from any rash actions. More figures emerged from the shadows and Kao saw that Albani was accompanied by a squadron of uniformed police officers. Their black uniforms, and the white sashes crossing their chests, identified them as carabinieri, members of a special corps of the Italian military who served as both military and civilian police.

"What's this all about, signore?" Kao asked. As far as he knew, his tracks were well covered. He made a point of not carrying out operations in the country in which he currently resided. Italian intelligence had nothing to charge him with. He nodded to his men, who backed off obediently.

Albani regarded him frostily. "I am afraid you are under arrest for the possession of stolen NATO documents." He reached out and plucked the rose from Kao's lapel. "We have reason to believe that the purloined information is contained within a microdot hidden inside this flower."

"But I bought this only moments ago!" he protested. "From a flower girl in the *Piazza di Trevi.*" He glanced back over his shoulder, searching for the irresistible young street nymph, but instantly realized that he was wasting his time. Kao knew a frame-up when he found himself in the middle of one. No doubt the curvaceous flower vendor was long gone. "I am a Chinese national," he informed Albani. "I demand to speak with my embassy."

"Of course," the man from National Security replied. He smirked as he handed the incriminating rose off to one of his underlings, who promptly deposited it in a plastic evidence bag. "I must warn you, however, that these are very serious charges. At the very least, you can expect to be deported immediately, unless you choose to assist us in another matter, in which case all this unpleasantness can be made to go away."

"I see," Kao said knowingly. So this was a shakedown, then. He wondered what Albani, or whomever he was working for, was after. "I'm listening."

Albani snapped his fingers, and another man stepped from the murky depths of a nearby doorway. Kao did not recognize the newcomer at first, but when the man removed his reflective sunglasses and peeled off a false mustache, Kao Yun knew at once who had engineered this entire sting after calling in some old favors owed him by his Italian colleagues. Jack Bristow joined Albani beneath the glow of the streetlights.

"What do you want, Jack?" Kao sighed wearily. He had crossed paths with the American operative before, although it had been several years since they had last met. *In Cairo,* he recalled, *during that business with nerve gas.* Kao had lost track of Bristow's true alliances since then; was he still affiliated with the CIA, or was he working freelance these days? *Obviously, I should have been watching him more closely.*

Jack glanced at the clear plastic bag containing the rose. "That was sloppy, Kao," he commented coolly. As always, his bland expression masked any hint of emotion. "Then again, you always did have a weakness for a pretty face. Remember that chorus girl in Shanghai?"

Kao didn't need the reminder. "I suspect you're not here to discuss ancient history. I ask again, what do you want?"

"Nothing much," Jack said, getting down to business. "I believe you may have dealt recently with one Niccolo Genovese, otherwise known as The Fire. I want you to arrange a meeting with his surviving partner, The Smoke."

"I have no idea what you're talking about," Kao said automatically. He was starting to wish he had never heard of The Fire or The Smoke. *What is Jack's involvement in this matter?* he wondered. Did Bristow have anything to do with that mysterious woman in London? Kao had heard certain rumors regarding Jack's daughter, who was supposed to take after him. He instantly compared the face of the duplicitous flower girl with the blonde in the bookshop's security footage. He didn't *think* they were the same woman.

"Now who is wasting time?" Jack said impatiently. "I'm not interested in you or your operations today. I'm after The Smoke, concerning another matter." He nodded at Albani, who beckoned the carabinieri forward. The Italian troopers appeared unintimidated by Kao's looming bodyguards, whom they outnumbered two to one. "It's in your own best interests to cooperate."

"They'll never make the charges stick," Kao argued. Nevertheless, he swallowed hard at the prospect of spending time in an Italian prison cell. "This is a transparent case of entrapment."

"Maybe," Jack conceded. "But it's more than enough to revoke your visa." His merciless eyes dissected the Chinese businessman. "I can't imagine you're in a hurry to report back to Beijing, not after your recent reverses."

He's got a point. Damn him, Kao admitted to himself. He was in enough hot water regarding the London fiasco. The last thing he needed now was to be exiled back to China with a scandal hanging over his head. Even if he tried to explain to his superiors what had actually transpired, he would just end up looking like a skirt-chasing idiot. His career would be over, along with his chances of living to a ripe old age.

"All right," he surrendered. "I'll see what I can do."

CHAPTER 6

MEXICAN CONSULATE

"'Two roads diverged in a yellow wood,'" Sydney read aloud, then put down the textbook. "What does Frost mean by that? In his poem 'The Road Not Taken,' he isn't just talking about a literal fork in the road. He's writing about the choices we make in our lives that determine where we ultimately end up. The diverging paths are a metaphor for the turning points in every life. But, of course, for every choice we make, every road we choose, there's another road that we never get to try. The road not taken."

Like teaching, she reflected. *That was one road I never followed to the end. Who knows where it might have led me? Assuming I was ever meant to be on that road to begin with.* "Do you see what I mean?"

"Sure," Mercedes mumbled without enthusiasm. "I guess."

The teenager was slumped behind a desk, staring blankly at the screen of her laptop. Encyclopedias and textbooks, in both Spanish and English, crammed the bookshelves lining the tiny classroom, and a framed map of the world was mounted on one wall. A dry erase board was available for Sydney to write on. Sydney's own desk faced her student's, but at the moment she preferred to stand as she discoursed on poetry and metaphor, walking back and forth between Mercedes and the board. She hoped her teacher act was convincing.

"What about you?" she asked Mercedes, hoping to engage the girl's interest. "Can you think of any points in your own life when you had to choose which road to take?"

"I wish!" She laughed bleakly at the question. "Like I have any say about what happens to me. You should be reading that dumb poem to my mom and stepdad. They're the ones who make all the decisions around here."

Sydney wasn't sure how to respond to that. Suspecting that a prudent tutor would want to avoid getting into the middle of any family disputes, she tried to steer the discussion back toward Robert Frost. "Well, what do you think the poem means by 'the road less traveled'? Do you think the narrator is recommending one choice over another?"

"I don't know," Mercedes said with a shrug. She refused to make eye contact with Syd and looked as though she would rather be anywhere else. Mexico City, maybe, where her friends were. Outside, a cold New York wind whipped around the corner of the brownstone. "You tell me."

Sydney felt exasperation setting in. So far, tutoring the sullen teenager was proving more of a challenge than infiltrating a terrorist training camp. "That's not the point," she said a bit impatiently. "The idea is to get *you* to think about the extraordinary possibilities of language. What does this poem mean to you?"

"Nothing much," Mercedes muttered. She kept her eyes glued to the screen of her laptop. Sydney circled around behind the girl and was not surprised to find a game of solitaire on the monitor, as opposed to the text of the poem. Resisting an urge to demonstrate her Krav Maga combat skills on the sullen teen, Syd reached out and closed the laptop.

"You're supposed to be concentrating on your lessons." Sydney winced at the hectoring tone in her voice. *Patience,* she counseled herself. *You've faced down terrorists and torturers. You can handle one hostile teenager.* "You can at least try to pay attention."

Mercedes was not at all apologetic or embarrassed at being caught playing a game on her computer. "Don't worry," she said sarcastically, "I'll tell my mom and stepdad that they're getting their money's worth. Not that they really care whether I learn anything. They just want me out of their hair for a couple of hours a day."

Was that a note of genuine pain beneath the hostility? Even though she was currently suffering the consequences of the teenager's bad attitude, Sydney felt a twinge of sympathy for Mercedes. After only two days at the consulate, Syd had already grasped that the girl's busy parents seemed to have little time for her. Ambassador Delgado was occupied with his diplomatic career, while Catalina was constantly off shopping or attending society functions with her hunky bodyguard in tow. No wonder Mercedes felt neglected. Syd had felt much the same way when she was little, after they thought her mother had died. Her father had thrown himself into his work, growing colder and more distant with each passing year. *It's not easy feeling like an orphan,* she recalled, *especially when your dad is still alive.*

Still, she liked to think that she had never taken it out on her teachers.

"I'm sure, in their own way, they only want what's best for you." She spotted the iPod looped around Mercedes's neck and tried another tack. "You like music, right? Well, can you think of any popular songs that use the same kind of metaphor? Something about roads or paths or choosing a direction?"

Mercedes considered the question for all of about fifteen seconds. "Nah."

Thanks for giving it plenty of thought, Sydney thought irritably. She clenched her fists in frustration. "Come on," she urged Mercedes. "Think about it. You must be able to come up with something."

"Give me a break!" Mercedes spat, glaring

rebelliously at Sydney. "This is all a big waste of time, anyway. What do I care what some old Anglo wrote a zillion years before I was born. Let it go, why don't you?"

"Sorry, that's not how it works," Sydney said firmly. Even though she felt sorry for Mercedes to a degree, she wasn't going to let the girl walk all over her. *I may be just a bogus teacher, but I'm going to stay in charge of my classroom.* "We're done here for today, but you're not off the hook yet." She walked over to the bookshelves and retrieved a hardcover copy of Dante's *Divine Comedy.* She dropped the heavy tome in front of Mercedes. "This book begins with the narrator lost in the woods. Before you report back here tomorrow, I want five thousand words comparing Dante's use of road imagery to 'The Road Not Taken.' And don't even think about downloading something from the Internet." She gave Mercedes a steely look. "Trust me, I've had a lot of experience exposing cheats."

For a second the girl wilted before Sydney's forbidding gaze. Then her adolescent attitude reasserted itself. "Yeah. Right. Whatever." She snatched up the book and her laptop and stormed out of the classroom, leaving Sydney alone with her doubts.

That went well, she thought bitterly, disappointed by her failure to get through to her one and only student. *Maybe I was never cut out to be a teacher after all.* She couldn't help recalling that her mother, who had been the original inspiration for Sydney's interest in education, had ultimately turned out to be a KGB assassin in disguise. *Perhaps, at the core, I'm more like Irina Derevko than Laura Bristow.*

A discouraging thought.

After her failure in the classroom, it was a relief to get back to some honest-to-goodness spying. At two in the morning, when the rest of the consulate was presumably asleep, Sydney used the bugs she had planted earlier to listen in on the offices on the third floor. All was silent, confirming that nobody on the staff was working into the wee hours of the morning. She was good to go.

"Phoenix to Shotgun," she notified Vaughn. "I'm on the move."

"Got that, Phoenix," he replied from across the street. "Good luck."

"Thanks!"

Slipping quietly out of her room, she tiptoed

toward the stairs. She padded softly down the corridor, past the rest of the servants' quarters. Infrared contact lenses allowed her to navigate the hall in the dark. In lieu of an all-black cat burglar's outfit, she wore a dark turtleneck and slacks, just in case she ran into somebody by accident. If caught, she planned to plead insomnia, or perhaps a case of the midnight munchies. There were plenty of books in the ambassador's office, she recalled. She could always claim she was just looking for something to read.

Those were worst-case scenarios, however. She had no intention of being caught.

Sydney took the stairs to the third floor, then went straight to Ambassador Delgado's office. The heavy oak door was locked for the night, but she easily picked it. Closing the door behind her, she crept into the office and started looking around. The glow of the streetlamps outside filtered through the curtains over the windows.

Where to begin? She wasn't sure exactly what she was searching for. She doubted that Delgado would have notes concerning his own assassination on file in his office. Still, the incriminating call had been made on the ambassador's private line, so it made sense to investigate. Besides, she might stumble onto something that would give them a better idea of who the man's enemies were. Death threats, perhaps, or a revised will. *At this point I can use all the intel I can get.*

Sydney started with the ambassador's desk. The drawers were locked, but they proved no match for Sydney's expertise. She quickly rifled through the files but spotted no obvious smoking guns. She found calendars and itineraries, copies of various UN resolutions and reports, invitations to charity events, special appeals from prominent Mexican businessmen with visa problems, résumés and requests for internships, correspondence with the Mexican consuls in D.C. and elsewhere, et cetera, et cetera. A draft of Delgado's upcoming presentation on drug trafficking caught her eye, reminding her that the ambassador's time was very possibly running out. She used a digital camera, hidden inside her wristwatch, to record the various documents for more in-depth analysis later. Perhaps Sloane or the rest of APO would notice something she had missed.

A glamour shot of Catalina rested atop the desk, not far from the photo of the orphanage.

Sydney didn't see any pictures of Mercedes. *Poor kid,* she thought. *Guess Delgado isn't the ideal stepdad after all.*

Putting the files back the way she found them, Sydney moved on to the framed painting of the cathedral. She checked first to make sure the Chicklets-size bug was still in place, then lifted the bottom of the frame. She half-expected to find a safe hidden behind the painting, but, alas, whoever had designed the office had been more imaginative. She carefully rehung the painting and pondered her next move. Should she search Rivera's office next or Allende's? What about Catalina's?

Before she could decide, a noise from the corridor outside sent a jolt of fear through her system. Alarmed, she turned toward the door in time to see the glare of a flashlight through the paper-thin gap between the door and the floor. A ghostly plane of light slid across the carpet.

Someone was coming.

"Phoenix to Shotgun! I have company!"

"Roger that, Phoenix." She could hear the anxiety in Vaughn's voice. "Do you require assistance?"

Charging uninvited into a foreign consulate would definitely be a diplomatic faux pas, yet

Sydney knew that Vaughn and Weiss wouldn't hesitate if they thought she was in genuine jeopardy. That was a last-ditch option, though, to be avoided if at all possible.

"I'll let you know."

Sydney sprang across the room to lock the door from the inside. A second later she heard someone fumbling with the doorknob. She held her breath, waiting to see if the newcomer would move on, but instead she heard the unmistakable sound of someone trying to jimmy the lock.

Who else was breaking into the ambassador's office tonight?

Sydney was curious, but not enough to let herself be caught by the intruder. Especially while unarmed. Looking around for an escape route, she immediately decided on the windows facing the street below. She rushed silently to the nearest window and ducked behind the curtains.

She quickly slid open the window. A gust of cold air invaded the office, causing the curtains to billow. Ignoring the frigid breeze, Sydney clambered out onto the window ledge, more than two stories above the sidewalk below. She balanced precariously on the narrow ledge and made sure her footing was solid. Holding on to the edge of the window frame with her right hand, she cautiously slid the glass pane closed again with her left—just as the door to the office swung open. She prayed that the curtains would fall still before the intruder turned his flashlight in her direction.

The winter wind chilled her. She shivered beneath her turtleneck, realizing that she was not dressed appropriately for February in New York. She clenched her jaw to keep her teeth from chattering.

Through a crack in the curtains, she watched the newcomer enter the office. Just as she had done moments ago, he quietly closed the door behind him before searching the room with his flashlight. Sydney ducked away from the incandescent beam, but not before catching a glimpse of the intruder's face through her infrared lenses.

It was Manuel Rivera.

What the hell? Sydney thought. What was the urbane young deputy doing in his boss's office at two thirty in the morning? She doubted he was there to get an early start on the next day's paperwork.

Unlike Sydney, Rivera ignored the desk and the artwork and headed for one of the rustic pine bookcases lining the walls of the office. He removed several volumes of bound policy papers, revealing a wall safe hidden behind the inconspicuous tomes. Sydney mentally kicked herself for not finding the safe first, then conceded that the ambassador's number one aide had a distinct advantage when it came to knowing where the bodies were buried. Judging from Rivera's furtive behavior, however, she guessed that the deputy was overstepping his boundaries a bit. He probably had no more right to mess with the safe than she did.

In the meantime, despite the fascinating scene unfolding in the office, Sydney was feeling more than a little exposed as she clung to the front of the old brownstone. At this time of night, there wasn't a whole lot of traffic—pedestrian or otherwise—on the street below, but it was only a matter of time before someone spotted a suspicious figure lurking on the window ledge, which could lead to a whole bunch of awkward questions that Iris Talbot was not prepared to answer. *I don't think Allende or the cops would buy that I was sleepwalking.*

"Hey, Shotgun," she whispered over her comm, "I could use a blackout right now."

"We're one step ahead of you, Phoenix," Vaughn informed her. A second later all the lights went out for blocks in every direction. The street-lamps went dark, casting the neighborhood into the sort of impenetrable blackness that the average New Yorker rarely encountered even on the murkiest of nights. "Thanks, Shotgun!" Sydney said.

"Don't thank me," Vaughn replied modestly. She assumed that he was watching her with night-vision binoculars from across the street. "Thank Merlin. He's the one who talked us through it while Houdini and I hacked into the city's power grid. We shut down the whole neighborhood."

Marshall broke into the conversation. "Nothing to it," he insisted. "To be honest, it was kind of fun. How often do you get to trigger a genuine New York blackout? I got to pretend I was a member of the Legion of Doom or something. The infamous '80s hackers, I mean, not the bad guys from *SuperFriends*, although that would be kind of cool too."

Sydney realized it was approaching midnight back in Los Angeles. "Thanks for working late, Merlin." She knew he had a wife and baby waiting for him at home. "You're a lifesaver, as usual."

Vaughn spoke urgently into her ear. She resisted the temptation to look over her shoulder at the darkened office across the street. "You'd better get out of there, Phoenix. Con Edison is trying to restore the power as we speak. I'm not sure how long this blackout will last."

Sydney appreciated his concern, but she wasn't ready to abandon her perch just yet. "Hold on for a sec. Turns out our late-night caller is Rivera. I want to see what he's up to."

"Roger, Phoenix." She could tell from Vaughn's voice that he wasn't happy she was stalling, but he knew better than to argue with her. "Just get ready to move the moment the lights come back on."

"You bet," she promised.

Turning her attention back to Rivera, she watched the skulking deputy employ a noiseless laser torch to drill into the reinforced steel housing of the safe. Clearly, the ambassador had not trusted him with the combination. Sydney monitored his progress, wondering what she should do if Rivera managed to get the safe open and tried to abscond with the contents. Would it be worth exposing herself to take possession of whatever he was after? Maybe if she crept up on him from behind, before he had a chance to identify her . . .

EEEEeeeeeeee!

A blaring alarm rendered the idea pointless. Rivera jumped back from the safe, which obviously had its own backup power source, and turned off his laser drill. Apparently his safecracking skills left something to be desired.

Amateur, she thought.

Thanks to the blackout, the consulate remained dark despite the earsplitting alarm. But Sydney heard agitated voices and stirring bodies throughout the building. Footsteps pounded on the stairs below, and she knew that Allende's men would be charging into the office within seconds. Rivera had the same realization and darted for the door. Sydney wondered how he expected to get away.

That's his *problem,* she concluded. She needed to get back to her own room, pronto, before anyone thought to check on the new tutor. "Phoenix to Shotgun. I'm out of here."

Vaughn wisely refrained from saying "I told you so."

Sydney glanced down at the sidewalk, two floors below. Jumping was not an option. The last thing she needed was to be lying on the pavement with a broken leg when the cop cars arrived. She could already hear the sirens converging on East 40th Street. The consulate was flush with the buildings on either side of it, so she couldn't creep around the brownstone to the fire escape at the rear, which left her with only one way to go: up.

Tipping her head back, she peered up at the rooftop, more than three stories above her. It was a long distance to climb, especially without any equipment, but the only alternative was staying put and getting arrested.

She took a deep breath, then edged along until she was clear of the window, with a broken stretch of reddish-brown brickwork stretching above her. She wiped her sweaty palms on her slacks, then experimentally probed the wall above her head, searching for holds in the crumbling mortar between the stones. She found a couple of gaps, and dug her fingers into them. Lifting one foot, she jammed the rubber sole of her sneaker flat against the wall and pushed upward.

The trick to free climbing, she recalled, is to rely on your leg muscles as much as possible, as opposed to your fingers and arms. Keeping this in mind, she began her ascent, using her hands to hold herself in place while propelling herself upward with her legs. She tried not to think about the paved sidewalk waiting for her if she slipped.

"Phoenix! What are you doing?" Vaughn asked tensely.

"Just what it looks like," she muttered, focusing on the bricks above her. She registered vaguely that someone had shut off the alarm inside the building.

"Are you out of your mind?" he protested.

Sydney imagined his horrified expression. "Don't worry," she assured him. "It's just like rock climbing out by Malibu."

Granted, without the benefit of any safety ropes.

By the time Sydney reached the top of the fourth floor, she was drenched in sweat. She wedged the toes of her sneakers into the gaps she had previously found with her hands. Gusts of winter wind threatened to blow her away from the wall, but she held on to the exterior of the brownstone for dear life, despite the cold that was turning her fingers numb. One hand at a time, she blew on her fingers to warm them.

I wonder if it's too late to call for a helicopter pickup, she thought.

Hand over hand, she scaled the brownstone. "Can you believe people actually do this for fun?" she asked Vaughn, mostly to keep her mind off the grisly consequence of a missed step or loose hold. "It's called 'buildering.' Sort of a pun on 'bouldering.' For people who like to climb the sides of skyscrapers and such."

"So I hear." Vaughn was unable to entirely hide the anxiety in his voice. "Me, I figure if God meant for us to climb up buildings on the outside, he wouldn't have given us elevators."

"At the moment, I'm inclined to agree," Syd admitted.

She managed to ascend in more or less a straight line until she hit the middle of the fifth floor. Then her luck ran out. Finding no suitable holds directly above her, she was forced to traverse horizontally along the face of the building until she located a crack in the mortar deep enough for her to sink her fingers into. It wasn't perfect, but it would have to do. Stretching to reach the hold, she grabbed the damaged brick, then pushed off with her right foot.

Old sandstone, weakened by decades of smog and acid rain, crumbled beneath the pressure, and her foot slipped free of the wall. Without its support, her other foot came loose as well, and Sydney found herself dangling by her fingertips. She bit down on her lip to keep from crying out.

"Sydney!" Vaughn gasped, breaking protocol.

Gravity tugged mercilessly on her fingers, and she felt every ounce of her trim one hundred twenty-five pounds. Her fingertips felt like they were on the verge of snapping. Visions of her own body, lifeless on the sidewalk below, raced through her brain.

She swung toward the wall, her unmoored feet searching desperately for a toehold in the grimy brickwork. She managed to catch her right foot onto the corner of a brick, then probed desperately with her other foot until it found a crack as well. With much apprehension, she transferred her weight to her legs, giving her fingers a break. To her relief, the bricks held.

She pressed herself against the sooty building, gasping for breath. *That was a close one!* Remembering Vaughn, she whispered into her comm. "Sorry about that. Hope I didn't give you a heart attack."

"Actually, you did," Vaughn answered. "Houdini just had to resuscitate me."

Sydney allowed herself a second to regain her composure, then looked up at the fifteen-plus feet of brick facade she still had to climb. She couldn't afford to waste any more time. She had to get back into the house. *It's not much farther,* she thought, giving herself a pep talk. *You can do it.*

She steadied her breathing and took off up the wall again. Her aching fingers felt like they had permanently frozen into hooklike claws. An overdose of adrenaline had her heart racing, while her mouth had gone dry. Her left leg started to cramp, and only sheer willpower kept it from jerking up and down like a sewing machine needle. Sydney's face was set in a mask of grim determination, her teeth clenched tightly. The wind whipped against her cheeks, leaving them raw and burning.

She passed the top of the fifth floor. Only one more story to go.

Red lights flashed beneath her as police cars pulled up to the curb in front of the consulate. Sydney didn't bother to look down. Why invite vertigo? She just hoped that nobody shone a flashlight in her direction.

"Phoenix," Vaughn said uneasily, "I don't want to rush you, but Con Ed's close to getting the power on. Those streetlamps will be lighting up any minute now!"

Damn! she thought. Once the lights went back on, someone was sure to spot her. "Hold them off as long as you can. Just a few more minutes!"

Pushing her luck, Sydney clambered rapidly up the last several feet. At the top of the sixth floor, however, a cornice blocked her path. Nearly a foot of solid limestone jutted out from the wall. *This is going to be tricky,* she thought, *but I've come too far to surrender now.*

Digging into the brickwork with both feet and five fingers, she leaned out away from the wall, tempting fate. She stretched her free arm as far as it would reach, straining her fingertips until—finally!—they cupped around the outer lip of the cornice. Without letting go of her other grips, she tugged experimentally on the protruding stone, testing its strength. Could it bear her full weight? It seemed secure enough, but there was only one way to find out for sure.

"If this doesn't work . . . it's not your fault," she whispered to Vaughn.

"Don't do it!" he pleaded. "It's too dangerous!"

"Tell my father I forgive him . . . for everything."

Just then the power came back on. Fortieth

Street lit up in an instant, suddenly blinding in the wake of the darkness. Sydney blinked against the sudden glare. Streetlamps illuminated the sidewalk, while more light poured from the windows of the consulate and the other nearby buildings. For three o'clock in the morning, there was a surprising number of people up.

Without a moment to lose, she let go of the wall. She swung out beneath the cornice, her feet once more dangling perilously in the air. Using the momentum of her swing, she grabbed on to the overhang with her other hand. A surge of elation burst through her veins as she felt all ten fingers take hold.

Now she had to rely on her upper body strength. Sydney silently gave thanks for every hour she'd spent doing chin-ups, as she laboriously pulled herself up and over the edge of the cornice. She dropped, panting, onto the tar papered rooftop. Steam rose from a ventilation shaft nearby, and a break in the cloud cover gave her a glimpse of a thin, crescent moon. "See," she teased Vaughn over the comm-link, "just like rock climbing in Malibu."

"I stand corrected," he said, relieved. "Now you'd better get a move on."

Sydney groaned. Exhausted, she wanted nothing more than to catch her breath for a few minutes, but she couldn't afford to take a break just yet. It was only a matter of time before someone checked on the new tutor, if they hadn't already. "I read you, Shotgun. I'm on my way."

Lurching to her feet, she sprinted across the rooftop toward the rear of the building, where a wrought iron fire escape led to the enclosed courtyard six stories below. She slid down a metal ladder and raced across an elevated steel platform until she reached her own window on the sixth floor. In a moment of foresight, she had left the window open a crack, just in case she needed to make a swift return via the fire escape. *Of course, I never figured I'd have to scale the front of the building first!*

She slid open the window and crept back into her room. To her relief, it looked just as she had left it. The lights were still off, and the door to the hallway was still locked. Lesson plans and homework were laid out conspicuously on the desk the consulate had provided for her. A dog-eared novel rested on an end table next to the bed, along with a pair of glasses and a reading lamp. The sheets were turned down and rumpled on her bed, as if she had been sleeping fitfully. The closet doors and bureau drawers were snugly shut, just as she had left them. The transparent tape stretched inconspicuously across the bottom of the door remained intact.

Whew! It looked like her cover hadn't been blown.

Sydney didn't have long to savor her safe return. An insistent knock at the door caused her to jump. "Ms. Talbot! Iris! Are you all right?" The voice sounded familiar, but she couldn't quite place it through the door. "Ms. Talbot!"

"Hold on!" she called back. Under the circumstances, she figured it couldn't hurt to sound flustered. "I'll be right with you!"

What with the break-in and all, Syd thought it best to pretend that she had been fast asleep when the alarm went off. To convey this impression, she kicked off her sneakers and slacks, then tugged her sweater down over her hips like a nightshirt. She punched her pillow, creating a deep indentation, then jumped on and off the bed. The wind outside had already messed up her hair, but she shook her head a few times just to be safe. She popped the infrared contact lenses into her palm and grabbed for her glasses.

Impatient knuckles rapped on the door once more. "Ms. Talbot!"

"I'm coming!" She gave the room a quick once-over to make sure it presented the right appearance for 3:15 A.M., and unlocked the door, which swung open to reveal Manuel Rivera—of all people—standing in the hallway outside. Sydney's muscles tensed, poised to go into combat mode if Rivera had come to confront her. Did he know she had been spying on him earlier, when he was trying to break into the ambassador's safe? Was he here to threaten her?

I would've thought he'd be long gone by now, she thought.

"Mr. Rivera?"

"Excuse me, Ms. Talbot," he said courteously. There was nothing at all adversarial about his manner. "Forgive me for disturbing you, but I'm afraid there's been an intruder. Someone apparently broke into the ambassador's office."

Sydney gasped in surprise. "Oh no! Is that what this was all about? I heard the alarm, of course, but I wasn't sure what I should do. And then the power went out! I was afraid that there was some sort of terrorist attack underway, so I just hid in my room." She feigned alarm. "Was anybody hurt? The ambassador? Mercedes?"

"Everyone is fine," he assured her, while sneaking a peek at her bare legs. "It appears to have been some sort of burglary attempt, possibly espionage-related." He shook his head ominously. "These are perilous times, as I'm sure a highly educated woman such as yourself must be aware. The ambassador has many enemies."

Syd wasn't going to pass up an opening like that. "Like whom?"

"Political rivals. Corrupt government officials. The big drug cartels." He shrugged his shoulders beneath his Armani jacket. "Ambassador Delgado has made it his life's work to root out our nation's enemies and bring them to justice. Such an enterprise is not always welcomed by those who have enriched themselves at the expense of our people."

True enough, she thought, although she had hoped for something a little more specific. "Anybody in particular?"

Rivera smiled cryptically. "That's nothing you need worry about," he assured her. "This was just an isolated incident." He took a step toward the doorway, as though hoping to be invited into her room, but Sydney did not step out of his way. "Still, I'm relieved to find you well. For a few moments there, while you were making your way to the door, I was afraid that the intruder might have taken you hostage."

"Don't be silly." She tugged on the hem of her sweater, trying to cover herself. "Who'd want to take me prisoner? I'm just the schoolteacher."

"Desperate men can resort to desperate measures," Rivera observed. He peered past Sydney's shoulder into her room, as though the hypothetical intruder he was referring to might still be lurking there. His eyes narrowed suspiciously. "Your window is open."

Sydney glanced over her shoulder to see the curtains billowing into the room. *Great!* she thought sarcastically. *I must not have closed it all the way.*

"I thought I heard footsteps on the fire escape," she explained. "But by the time I got to the window, there was no one there."

"I see," he said thoughtfully. Sydney couldn't tell if he believed her or not. "The burglar escaping, surely."

Not likely, she thought, *considering that the*

only intruders were the two of us. But did Rivera know that? She couldn't resist putting him on the spot. "Say," she asked, glancing at her wristwatch, "what are you doing here at three o'clock in the morning?"

Rivera didn't miss a beat. "I keep a cot in my office, for when I'm working late. I must have dozed off. The next thing I knew, the burglar alarm was going off and there were security guards charging up the stairs. Imagine my surprise and disorientation!"

Yeah, right, Syd thought, although she kept her skepticism to herself. She still wanted to know what Rivera was after in the ambassador's safe. The polished young deputy was obviously up to no good. She made a mental note to have APO run a comprehensive background check on Manuel Rivera.

I want to know what he's hiding.

CHAPTER 7

UNITED NATIONS HEADQUARTERS
MANHATTAN

Nearly two hundred flags, representing all 191 Member States, were arrayed along the front of the six-block-long United Nations complex. Beyond the panoply of brightly colored flags, the glass-and-marble tower of the Secretariat building rose above the East River, dwarfing the domed General Assembly building just north of it. The Secretariat looked like an enormous, green-tinted slab beneath the clear morning sky. Unlike the rest of New York's skyscrapers, the thirty-nine-story building stood by itself, with acres of open space surrounding it, so that it reigned supreme along this stretch of the riverfront.

Marcus Dixon admired the striking modernist architecture as he approached the UN along First Avenue. His official UN grounds pass was clipped to his double-breasted winter coat. He warmed his hands around a steaming cup of coffee he had just purchased at a Korean deli. As it was only 8:32 A.M., he still had plenty of time before he had to report to his post in the conference building behind the General Assembly, so he strolled leisurely along the sidewalk. The air was brisk and invigorating.

As cover stories went, his present alias as a UN interpreter suited him. He had great respect for the United Nations' humanitarian and diplomatic efforts throughout the world, even as he recognized that sometimes more shadowy measures were required to preserve the peace and security of the world's peoples. Still, he liked to think that the CIA (and therefore APO) were ultimately working toward the same goal as the United Nations: a planet free from fear. He would not have devoted his life to U.S. intelligence—and endured countless sacrifices—if he didn't believe that.

He just wished his present assignment had

been more productive so far. Although his newly assumed position as the Mexican delegation's French and Russian interpreter had afforded him an excellent opportunity to observe Ambassador Delgado and his staff at work, he had made little progress in uncovering the delegation's connection to Niccolo Genovese. Nor had he discovered any real leads on who might want the ambassador dead.

From what he had gathered, Victor Delgado was respected and well liked by his fellow diplomats. He served diligently on a number of prominent UN commissions, including those on economic development in Latin America, human rights, and criminal justice. Today, for instance, he was expected to attend a meeting of the Advisory Committee on Sustainable Development, as well as a gathering of the Permanent Forum on Ecological Diversity. Dixon rather doubted that he would derive any useful intel from translating those sessions for the ambassador. Only Delgado's upcoming report to the UN Commission on Narcotic Drugs seemed likely to inspire an assassination plot against him, and even that was sheer speculation on Dixon's part.

I hope this isn't a wild goose chase, he thought

glumly. He missed his kids, who were at home with their babysitter in Los Angeles. Being separated from Robin and Steven was hard on him, especially now that their mother was dead, but he could endure it if he thought he stood a chance of eliminating a genuine threat. Still, he hated to think that he might be missing precious days of their childhood for no reason.

To his surprise, he also found himself missing Hayden Chase, certainly more than he had anticipated. The formidable CIA director was the first and only woman he had been with since his wife died, and their clandestine romance was still in its early stages, yet he couldn't help wishing that they could somehow arrange to rendezvous here in New York, as imprudent as that would be. *Where is this relationship going?* he thought. *Perhaps, after this mission is over, we'll have some time to find out. . . .*

He wondered how Sydney was faring at the consulate. He would have to check in with Vaughn and Weiss later on, perhaps during his lunch break. *Let's hope she's making more progress than I am.*

Tour groups were already lined up at the visitors' gate outside the General Assembly building.

Across the street, on the other side of First Avenue, demonstrators brandished placards and petitions protesting everything from the war in Iraq to global warming. Despite the chilly weather, the protestors seemed determined to bring their assorted issues to the attention of the international community. Busy joggers and commuters moved quickly past the activists, completely unfazed. Such demonstrations were nothing new here.

As a UN interpreter, albeit one with fraudulent credentials, Dixon bypassed the lines of tourists and kids on field trips and went through the staff entrance at 46th Street and First Avenue. "Good morning, Mr. Banks," a guard in a blue uniform greeted Dixon after checking his pass and waving him through the metal detector. "Have a nice day."

"Thanks," Dixon said, as though he had nothing more on his mind than another slate of multilingual committee meetings. An accredited UN interpreter was required to speak at least three of the UN's six official languages. For an agent of Dixon's experience, this posed little problem. "You too."

He approached the Assembly building on his way to the Conference building overlooking the East River. Technically, he was no longer on

American soil; by agreement, the UN grounds were international territory, another reason the CIA could not become involved in this affair directly. The landscaped plaza in front of the main entrance was already full of diplomats, journalists, and their aides going about their business. He was about to enter the building when an unexpected sight stopped him in his tracks.

Only a few yards away Arvin Sloane stood in the plaza, conversing with various officials.

As always, Dixon's mood darkened at the sight of Sloane. It was Sloane who had ordered Dixon's wife murdered, and he was behind any number of other atrocities. Even though nearly four years had passed since Diane's death by car bombing, Dixon had never come close to forgiving Sloane for his crimes, nor did he ever expect to. Sloane claimed to have reformed, but Dixon didn't believe it for a second. The number one reason he remained at APO, reporting to the same man who had made him a widower, was to keep watch over Sloane—and to be there when, inevitably, the man's true colors were revealed once more.

He knew Sydney felt much the same way.

But what was Sloane doing here, in New York,

at the United Nations? Dixon recognized the well-dressed men and women conferring with Sloane as high-ranking members of the Economic and Social Council. Did they realize, he wondered, that they were casually chatting with a man who had once been on the CIA's most wanted list? *Before he was pardoned, of course,* Dixon thought bitterly.

He did his best not to stare at Sloane, but for a moment they made eye contact with each other. A chill ran down his spine and a knot of righteous fury twisted deep within his gut. Sloane's lean, weathered face offered no clue as to what he was thinking.

Part of Dixon wanted to demand an immediate explanation from Sloane, but the professional in him knew better than that. He couldn't risk blowing his cover by revealing that they knew each other. *I need to contact APO,* he decided. *I have to find out why Sloane is here.* He glanced at his watch. He still had fifteen minutes before he was needed at the session on Indigenous Issues.

He looked around for someplace he could talk in private. The gardens north of the General Assembly building caught his eye and he headed for the rows of sycamores and oaks. Given the chilly temperature, he figured the gardens would be fairly empty this morning.

His assumption proved correct. Finding a secluded corner, he sat down on a bench and looked around to make sure no one was listening. Before he could activate his comm, however, his cell phone rang. He fished the phone from his pocket and checked the caller ID. It was Sloane.

"Yes?" he said, answering the phone. He kept his deep voice steady and under control, as he always did when conversing with APO's insidious director.

"Hello, Marcus." Sloane's congenial tone grated on Dixon's nerves. Among the man's most galling traits was his tendency to feign a close personal relationship with those he had betrayed. Sydney tried to hide it, but you could see her flinch whenever Sloane tried to act like a benevolent uncle with her. "I imagine you were surprised to see me just now."

"With reason," Dixon said coolly. "I thought you were in Los Angeles. Has there been some change to the mission parameters I should be aware of?"

"Not at all. As it happens, I was already scheduled to visit the United Nations on a matter unrelated to our present investigation." In fact, Sloane seldom ventured into the field these days, preferring to spin his webs from his command center in the APO bunker. "The World Food Programme is presenting me with an award on the eighth, in recognition of my past humanitarian efforts."

Sloane, after receiving his pardon, had headed an international relief organization known as Omnifam. Ostensibly intended to promote cancer research and combat world hunger, Omnifam had ultimately proven to be part of Sloane's master plan to locate his long-lost daughter, Nadia. Apparently, the United Nations remained unaware of the ulterior motive behind Sloane's charitable endeavors.

Bile rose at the back of Dixon's throat at the prospect of Arvin Sloane, traitor and mass murderer, being honored as a humanitarian.

He deserves a lethal injection, not an award for humanitarianism.

"I see." He could not bring himself to congratulate Sloane. "And why was I not informed of this?"

"As I said, it was irrelevant to your present assignment." His voice took on a frostier tone. "I do not owe you a full account of my outside activities, Marcus. This call was merely a courtesy."

Dixon imagined the severe expression on Sloane's face. "Frankly, I neglected to mention the award around the office because I rather suspected that certain individuals, yourself included, might find the subject distasteful."

"Perhaps," Dixon conceded. "But your unexpected appearance could have compromised my cover."

"Only if you were less than the professional I know you to be." Despite the praise, Sloane's voice held not a trace of warmth. "You may return to your mission, Agent Dixon. I expect results in a timely manner. Do not disappoint me."

Sloane broke off the call abruptly.

Dixon stared grimly at the silent phone before rising from the bench and heading back toward the General Assembly building. The morning air suddenly seemed much colder, and he replayed his strained conversation with Sloane over and over again in his head. Sloane's explanation for his presence did not sit right with Dixon, and not just because of the appalling notion of Arvin Sloane being honored by the United Nations. Vague suspicions followed Dixon into the lobby of the building and up the ramp leading to the second floor.

Is Sloane's arrival at the UN just a coincidence? he wondered. *Or is he making us all his pawns somehow?*

Dixon suspected the latter but knew he had to be careful before he made any rash accusations. He had already jumped the gun once before, when he'd tried to prove to Director Chase that Sloane was conspiring with former members of the Alliance, a series of criminal organizations that profited greatly from selling weapons, technology, and narcotics on the black market. Dixon had been proven wrong in that instance, and his attempt to catch Sloane in the act had nearly gotten Jack Bristow killed.

I'm not going to make that mistake again.

Nevertheless, part of Dixon prayed that APO's scheming director was lying to them once again, so that he could finally bring Arvin Sloane down once and for all.

In the meantime, he went back to work.

CHAPTER 8

MEXICAN CONSULATE

Sydney was pissed.

She strode down the corridor toward Catalina's office. Ramon stood guard outside the door, but Sydney brushed past him without explanation. She found the ambassador's wife seated behind an antique Spanish Colonial desk, inspecting the screen of an open laptop while simultaneously filing her ruby red nails. A framed poster from one of Catalina's movies occupied a position of honor on the eastern wall of the room. Unlike her husband's office, there were few bookcases and even fewer books. Instead, crystal and porcelain knickknacks occupied the available shelves. A vase of imported roses adorned her desk.

Catalina, wearing a white Halston suit that showed off her figure, looked up in surprise at Sydney's abrupt entrance. "Iris?"

"We need to talk about your daughter," Sydney said solemnly. Her grim expression made it clear that this was no joking matter.

Catalina sighed wearily. Sydney guessed she'd heard this before.

"Please sit down," the former starlet said, gesturing toward an antique wingback chair in front of the desk. She kept one eye on her laptop. "Do you mind if I sort through my e-mail as we speak? It's all I can do to keep up with my correspondence."

Sydney would have preferred Catalina's undivided attention, but she chose not to argue. She was relieved just to find the other woman in her office; Syd had discovered over the past couple of days that it could be difficult to catch Catalina between her spa dates and social engagements. "No problem. I know all about multitasking."

And then some.

Catalina languidly manipulated her mouse

while looking over the top of the screen at Sydney. The distinctive scent of Chanel wafted through the air between them. "Now then, what's this about my daughter?"

"I assigned Mercedes a five-thousand-word essay on the poetic use of road imagery," Sydney informed the other woman. "This is what she just handed in."

She thrust several sheets of notebook paper at Catalina. Mercedes's completed homework consisted of a single sentence, "This is a Dead End," repeated one thousand times.

"Caramba!" Catalina muttered, shaking her head as she flipped through the pages. "My apologies, Iris. I know that Mercedes can be . . . difficult . . . at times."

Tell me about it, Sydney thought. Despite her irritation, however, there was a positive side to Mercedes's defiance, in that it had given Sydney an excuse to track down Catalina and get to know her better. Although Rivera was definitely at the top of her list of suspicious characters since his aborted attempt to break into the ambassador's safe, Sydney still hadn't ruled out Catalina as a suspect when it came to the Genovese connection.

"Perhaps you can talk to Mercedes?" she suggested.

"I can try," Catalina said dubiously. "It's just so hard to get through to her these days." She threw up her hands. "Teenage girls. What can you do?"

Sydney recalled the bug she had planted in this very office days ago. So far, audio surveillance had not turned up anything incriminating. *Catalina could be totally innocent,* Syd reminded herself. *Not all younger wives want their husbands dead.*

And not all mothers are KGB assassins in disguise.

"Maybe a meeting among the three of us would help?" Sydney proposed, still playing the role of concerned teacher. Even if Mercedes's stunt had not ticked her off, she would have felt obliged to complain to the girl's parents, if only to stay in character. "Ideally, the ambassador could attend as well."

Catalina shook her head. "I don't know where we'd find the time. Our schedules are so demanding these days." She continued to click through her e-mail. "Still, if you really think it's important, I suppose I might be able to squeeze an hour or so into my calen—"

She halted in midsentence, caught off guard by

something she found in her e-mail. From where she was sitting, Sydney was unable to see the laptop's screen, but she couldn't miss Catalina's reaction. The older woman's eyes bulged from their sockets and her jaw dropped open. Her tanned complexion went pale as all the blood drained from her face. She clicked on an attachment, then clasped her hands to her mouth to hold back a horrified gasp. *"Madre de Dios!"*

"Mrs. Delgado . . . Catalina, what's wrong?" Sydney leaped from her seat and hurried around the desk in hopes of finding out what had provoked the other woman's dismay. But Catalina was too fast for her. She slammed down the lid of the laptop before Sydney could catch a glimpse of the screen. *Damn,* Sydney thought. "What's the matter? Is there anything I can do to help?"

"No! . . . No, thank you." Catalina hastily disconnected the laptop from its power cord. She snatched up the computer and held it tightly to her chest. Syd could see that her entire body was shaking. "I'm sorry," she stammered, stumbling to her feet. She acted like she was in shock. "I can't talk about this right now. . . . I have to go. . . ." She barely looked at Sydney, her mind suddenly elsewhere. It seemed to require a major effort just to interact with Sydney at all. "Something's come up. . . . I'm sorry. . . ."

She staggered out of the office in a daze, leaving Sydney behind. At the door, Ramon took one look at Mrs. Delgado's expression and went into guardian mode. "Catalina!" he exclaimed, and Sydney took note of the familiarity. Was it possible that the brawny bodyguard had a more than professional interest in the ambassador's wife? "What is it?" he entreated her. "Tell me."

Aware that other people were watching, Catalina pulled herself together. "It's nothing," she insisted with artificial good cheer. She continued to hold on to her laptop as though she half-expected it to turn and bite her. "I just need some air. Perhaps a drive would clear my head."

"Yes, senora," Ramon said, playing along. A worried expression remained on his square features. He eyed Catalina with obvious concern. "I'll call for a car."

Sydney watched them depart while her mind processed this puzzling new development. Suddenly Manuel Rivera wasn't the only one acting suspiciously. *What was that all about?* she wondered. *I should notify Vaughn and the others, pronto. I think we need to put Senora Delgado under tighter surveillance.*

"Phoenix to Shotgun," she whispered into her comm. "Grab your car keys. You're going for a ride."

EAST 40TH STREET
MANHATTAN

"How come you always get to drive?" Weiss griped.

Seated behind the wheel of a tan Subaru Forester, Michael Vaughn kept his eyes on the front steps of the Mexican Consulate. The Subaru was parked across the street from the brownstone, ready to roll as soon as their targets hit the road. An icy rain fell from ominous black clouds, forcing him to keep his window rolled down to keep the entrance to the consulate in view. "Because you couldn't win a coin toss if your life depended on it," Vaughn told his friend.

"That's because you won't let me use any of my trick coins," Weiss observed. The stocky agent occupied the passenger seat next to Vaughn. He rifled through a deck of playing cards as he spoke, practicing his sleight of hand. "Besides, we both know you're a control freak."

Vaughn was about to object to that characterization when their targets came into view. Just as Sydney had promised, Catalina Delgado emerged from the consulate, accompanied by a hulking bruiser dressed in black. *That must be Ramon,* Vaughn assumed. The bodyguard looked impatiently down the street while the ambassador's wife dabbed at her eyes with a tissue. A canvas awning protected them from the rain while they waited for their car. Syd had informed him and Weiss, via comm-link, of Catalina's mysterious breakdown and her subsequent plans to go for a drive. "Heads up," he alerted his partner. "There they are."

Within minutes a black Cadillac limousine with diplomatic plates pulled up to the curb in front of the consulate. Vaughn watched intently as Ramon dismissed the driver. Opening an umbrella, the bodyguard helped Catalina into the passenger seat, then got behind the wheel himself. Tinted windows concealed both Ramon and his charge from Vaughn's scrutiny. *Too bad we don't have a bug in the limo,* he thought.

The Cadillac pulled away from the curb and headed west on 40th Street. Vaughn hit his turn signal and counted to ten. Giving the Caddy a small head start, he began to merge into traffic. A horn blared loudly behind him, and he slammed on his brakes just as a gray Chevrolet Impala barreled past him, coming between him and the limo. *Asshole,* Vaughn thought irritably. He hated pushy New York drivers.

"Watch it, Speed Racer," Weiss teased him. "Getting into a fender bender would definitely put a cramp in our style."

"It wasn't my fault," Vaughn muttered, unamused. Fortunately, Manhattan gridlock being what it was, Catalina's limo hadn't gotten too far ahead of them. He pulled out into traffic and took off in discreet pursuit of the Cadillac. Despite the inclement weather, the city streets were as crowded as ever. And it wasn't even rush hour yet. He rolled up the window to keep out the cold.

"Shotgun to Phoenix," he said. "Rolling surveillance in progress."

"Good luck," Sydney replied. It had been her idea to shadow Catalina and her bodyguard on this particular excursion. "I'm dying to know where she needed to go in such a hurry, especially after getting freaked out by that mystery e-mail."

Let's find out, he thought.

The limo turned right onto Madison Avenue, heading uptown. Vaughn followed, taking care to keep a couple of cars between them for anonymity's sake.

Navigating heavy traffic in foul weather, while also keeping the limo in view, required Vaughn's complete concentration. Speeding taxis darted from lane to lane with reckless abandon as impatient jaywalkers bolted across the street without warning. Horns blared at every intersection and with every signal change. The rain turned potholes into puddles. The Subaru's windshield wipers worked overtime to allow Vaughn to see where he was going. The downpour was a double-edged sword, he realized, hiding the Subaru from their quarry but also making it harder to keep the limo in view.

"So, what do you think has the ambassador's missus so spooked?" Weiss asked, making conversation. He fanned out the playing cards, then shuffled them back together.

"Nothing she wants anyone to find out about," Vaughn said harshly. A scowl twisted his lips and his eyes narrowed suspiciously. "Chances are, Ambassador Delgado has no clue what his wife's been up to. The husbands never do."

Weiss shot him a wary glance. "Whoa there, buddy. Projecting much?"

Vaughn's scowl deepened. He knew what his

friend was alluding to. It had been little more than a year since Vaughn's own wife had betrayed him, spying on the CIA for the Covenant while simultaneously carrying on a sordid affair with Julian Sark. Vaughn had evened the score by killing Lauren before she could kill Sydney, but the wounds left by his wife's treachery still festered within his soul. *But I can put that behind me when I have to.*

Can't I?

"That has nothing to do with this," he insisted. "I'm just saying that she obviously has something to hide."

"Yeah, right," Weiss said. He sounded unconvinced of Vaughn's absolute objectivity. "Just remember who you're talking to, pal. I know you better than that." He sat up straight in his seat. "Hang on! They're turning right."

Momentarily distracted by thoughts of Lauren, Vaughn had almost missed the limo turning right onto 69th Street. *Damn it,* he thought, cursing himself for his inattention. He switched lanes rapidly and followed the Cadillac onto the busy cross street. For a second he was afraid he had lost the limo, but then he saw it disappearing through the gate of a multilevel parking garage.

Now what? He briefly considered following the limo into the garage, but decided that would be too risky; Ramon and Catalina might realize they were being tailed. Instead he double-parked outside the garage's exit, waiting to see if the couple would emerge on foot. "Keep your eyes out for them," he instructed Weiss, who gave him a *duh* expression in return. His foot tapped impatiently against the floor of the car.

"Maybe she wanted to do a little shopping?" Weiss speculated, making a valid point. This part of the Upper East Side was a mecca for upscale shoppers. Prada, Gucci, Versace, and any number of other pricy designer shops were all within walking distance.

Vaughn shook his head. "Sydney is convinced that something fishy is going on."

"That's good enough for me, I guess." Weiss settled back into his seat. "I wouldn't want to bet against your girlfriend's instincts. Sydney's as good as they come." Over the years he had become a good friend to Sydney as well as Vaughn. "Of course, Nadia's no slouch either. Did I tell you about Belize? You should have seen—"

"Hold on," Vaughn interrupted him, as a familiar-looking gray Chevrolet cruised past them, slowing as it went by the front of the parking garage. "Isn't that the same Chevy that nearly slammed into us back on Fortieth?"

"Maybe," Weiss said. "You think they're tailing us?"

"I think they're tailing *somebody*." Their last encounter with the Chevy had been more than thirty blocks ago. What were the odds that the car just happened to be going the same way as both the Subaru and the limo? "You keep watching for our targets. I want to see if it comes by again."

Was somebody else shadowing the ambassador's wife? Activating his comm, he brought Sydney up to date on the latest developments. "Looks like we may have competition."

"You're kidding," she answered. He could hear the curiosity in her voice. "Catalina's more popular than I realized."

"So it appears," he agreed.

Sure enough, a few minutes later the gray Chevy reappeared, having apparently circled around the block. "Bingo," Vaughn said, inspecting the car more closely this time. The driver appeared to be a middle-aged Hispanic man with a pockmarked face and a short military haircut. Vaughn memorized the Chevy's license plate number as it approached the parking garage one more time.

"Red alert," Weiss announced. "Targets back in view. They've switched cars."

Looking away from the Chevy, Vaughn saw a somewhat battered-looking green Hyundai Elantra exit the parking garage. Ramon was at the wheel with Catalina right beside him. Vaughn guessed that the Cadillac was parked somewhere inside the garage.

Shopping trip my ass, he thought. Nobody trades in a limo for a Hyundai unless they're trying to avoid being noticed or followed. The Hyundai turned left onto Park Avenue, and Vaughn waited to see what the gray Chevy would do.

It turned left as well.

"That clinches it," he said aloud. "We have another player in the game."

Weiss whistled slowly. "Who do you think it is?"

"Hell if I know," Vaughn said grimly. Hitting the gas, he took off after the other two vehicles. Within minutes they were cruising uptown behind the Chevy, which in turn was tailing the Hyundai. Taxis and other random automobiles broke up the procession.

"Wow," Weiss murmured, "it's a spy parade."

Vaughn was less inclined to see the humor in the situation. Keeping the Hyundai in view, he opened up a line to Marshall. "Shotgun to Merlin," he intoned soberly. "I need you to run a license number for me. It's for a gray Chevrolet with New York plates."

"No problem," Marshall declared. "Sock it to me."

Vaughn rattled off the number, then had Marshall read it back to him. "That's it," he confirmed. "I need that info as soon as you can get it."

"Okay, Shotgun." He could hear Marshall clicking away at his keyboard. "Got it! That vehicle is registered to Montezuma Protection Services, a private security firm based out of Manhattan."

Who? Vaughn had never heard of Montezuma Protection before. What was their stake in this? "Find out what you can about this Montezuma outfit, okay? I want to know whose side they're on."

"I'm on it," Marshall promised from more than three thousand miles away. "Just give me a few minutes."

The covert caravan continued north on Park Avenue. At 96th Street, ritzy shops, museums, and exorbitantly expensive apartment buildings abruptly gave way to low-rent tenements, as the Upper East Side transformed into El Barrio, or Spanish Harlem. Colorful graffiti was splashed on the walls of the tenements and public housing. Vaughn recalled that East Harlem had been the heart of New York's Hispanic community for more than fifty years, welcoming successive generations of immigrants from Puerto Rico, Mexico, the Dominican Republic, and elsewhere.

Led by the Hyundai, the cars turned right onto a main drag populated by Mexican restaurants, record shops, and stores displaying piñatas, cheap electronics, and *fútbol* jerseys. Most of the signs in the windows of the businesses were in Spanish. From there, the procession headed into a modest residential neighborhood that appeared to be relatively graffiti-free. Black-painted fire escapes climbed the facades of various red and blue apartment buildings. The freezing rain, which was now coming down in sheets, had cleared the sidewalks, making the neighborhood appear strangely deserted, although a steady stream of traffic continued to roll down the one-way street. The vehicles on the road were mostly personal autos and delivery trucks, as the previously ubiquitous yellow cabs seemed to have eschewed East Harlem for the more affluent territory below 96th Street.

The Hyundai slowed and parked by the curb, but only Ramon got out of the car. He pulled the collar of his jacket over his head to shield himself from the rain. Driving slowly down the street, a few cars behind the enigmatic gray Chevy, Vaughn watched as Ramon hurried down the block until he came to what looked like a converted tenement building. A sign in one of the upper windows of the building read APARTMENTS FOR RENT. The bodyguard looked up and down the streets suspiciously, then drew some keys from his pocket and went inside the redbrick building without Catalina, who was presumably waiting back in the car. Vaughn found it odd that the bodyguard would leave his glamorous charge alone.

The gray Chevy drove past the building as though Ramon's activities were of no interest to its short-haired driver. It rounded the corner at the end of the block, briefly vanishing from Vaughn's view. He guessed that it wasn't going far now that the Hyundai had apparently arrived at its destination. It occurred to Vaughn that the green car from the parking garage looked less conspicuous in this neighborhood than the limousine would have.

Vaughn still had time to park the Subaru on the same block as the apartment building. He clicked on his turn signal and pulled up to the curb next to a vacant lot across the street and a few buildings ahead of the redbrick domicile Ramon had entered. Weiss rolled down his window to give them a clear view of the front of the former tenement, and cold air invaded the Subaru. "Hey, check that out," Weiss said, nudging Vaughn. Ramon appeared briefly in one of the second-floor windows. He scanned the street below while talking on his cell phone, then drew the curtains shut.

A few minutes later Catalina came rushing down the sidewalk, beneath the shelter of the umbrella Ramon had chivalrously left with her. Had he called to tell her the coast was clear, or did she just want to avoid being seen entering the building with the buff, young bodyguard? A designer scarf was tied over her golden hair and, despite the stormy clouds overhead, dark sunglasses hid her eyes. Like Ramon, she paused on the stoop of the apartment building to look about furtively, before closing her umbrella and stepping inside.

"She couldn't look more guilty if she tried,"

Vaughn snarled, suspecting the worst of the ambassador's wife. "The only question is whether she's into assassination, adultery, or both."

Weiss sighed. "You're going to make me spell it out, aren't you? Before you get carried away, you need to remember one thing: Catalina Delgado is *not* Lauren."

"I know that!" Vaughn snapped.

"Hey, don't bite my head off!" Weiss held up his hands to ward off Vaughn's short temper. "I'm just trying to keep you honest, man. Provide a much needed reality check, you know?"

Vaughn took a deep breath, calming himself. His friend meant well. And who knew? Maybe Weiss had a point. But that whole fiasco with Lauren would have messed with anyone's head. Sometimes Vaughn still expected her to come back for revenge, even though he had seen her dead body lying on a slab in a top-secret CIA morgue. . . .

"Hey, at least I'm not dating a girl whose mother once tried to kill me," he quipped to lighten the mood. It was true; while being chased by the CIA, Irina Derevko had shot Weiss in the throat, nearly killing him. "How twisted is that?"

"That was years ago, dude! Ancient history."

Weiss spotted something outside the car and nodded at the sidewalk across the street. "Time out, pal. Look who's back."

Vaughn spotted the nameless driver from Montezuma Protection Services standing outside the apartment building, heedless of the pouring rain. His right hand was cupped over his ear, as though he was listening to instructions over some sort of comm-link. Vaughn guessed that the gray Chevy was parked around the corner somewhere. He slumped down in his seat to avoid being seen. Weiss did the same.

"You think he's onto us?" Weiss asked, watching the driver.

"No," Vaughn said, although he couldn't be sure. "Looks like he's focused on Catalina and Ramon, just like we are."

The driver nodded in response to an unknown voice, then continued down the block toward the now-empty Hyundai.

Vaughn made a snap decision. "You get out and follow that guy," he told Weiss. "See what he's up to. I'll stay here to watch for Catalina and Ramon."

"Sounds like a plan," Weiss agreed. He opened his door and casually stepped out onto the street. "It's raining pretty hard out here. We need an ark, not a Subaru." He checked to make sure his comm was still linked to Vaughn's. "Don't leave without me, okay?"

"I'll think about it," Vaughn teased his friend. "Now get going."

Weiss trotted away, leaving Vaughn alone to contemplate the apartment tenement, which seemed worlds away from the tony addresses Senora Delgado usually frequented. His smoldering gaze remained fixed on the curtained second-floor window. What were Catalina and Ramon doing up there? Despite Weiss's cautionary advice, Vaughn felt certain that the ambassador's wife and her husky bodyguard were having a clandestine affair. But what else was going on? Where did that e-mail fit in, and who else was shadowing the couple?

"Merlin to Shotgun, Phoenix," Marshall's voice piped up over the comm. "Have I got news for you! I thought you both ought to hear this."

"We're reading you, Merlin," Sydney replied. It sounded as though she were right there in the car with Vaughn.

No such luck, he thought. "What's up?"

"I did some research on Montezuma Protection Services, like you asked. And guess what?"

Marshall paused for dramatic effect. "Turns out the principal stockholder and founder of MPS is one Carlos Allende."

"The consulate's security chief?" Vaughn asked.

"The very same," Marshall answered. "Seems Allende has been moonlighting in the private sector, at least as a silent partner. It's unclear how involved he is with the firm on a day-to-day basis, but there's definitely a connection."

"Interesting," Sydney said. Vaughn recalled that she had already had at least one tense run-in with Allende. "It's starting to seem like everyone at the consulate is up to something."

I'll say, Vaughn thought. Was Catalina being blackmailed? Was she plotting to have her husband killed? Or all of the above?

After Lauren, he wouldn't be at all surprised to find out that the ambassador's wife was at the bottom of all of this.

CHAPTER 9

MEXICAN CONSULATE

"Good work, Merlin," Sydney said gratefully over her comm. She was back in her room on the sixth floor of the consulate, with her laptop open on her desk. Marshall's news about Carlos Allende's connection to the man following Catalina added a puzzling new wrinkle to an already complicated situation. Was Allende working in cahoots with Manuel Rivera, or was that a completely different conspiracy? And what did any of this have to do with the late Niccolo Genovese?

She massaged her forehead, trying to jump-start

her brain. On the screen of her portable computer, the official Web site for Montezuma Protection Services offered no clues as to Allende's true agenda. She was impressed that Marshall had managed to somehow extract the fact of Allende's silent partnership from the electronic ether.

Which reminded her . . .

"Merlin," she addressed him. "At the risk of pushing our luck, have you had any success with that other project we talked about?" While the guys had been trailing Catalina from Midtown to East Harlem, Sydney had asked Marshall to try to hack into Catalina's personal e-mail account. The image of the other woman's horrified expression was still fresh in Sydney's memory. Maybe Marshall could find out just what sort of e-correspondence had sent such a shock through Catalina's system—and caused her to go rushing up to El Barrio with Ramon in tow. "I realize we've been keeping you pretty busy."

"Please!" he protested vigorously, as though offended by the notion that he might have too much on his plate. "It's not like you asked me to find a back door into the Project Black Hole mainframe or something. I've been finessing her passwords and firewalls even as we speak, and with a remarkable degree of success, I might add. You'd think an ambassador's wife would rate better security than this. My ten-year-old niece in Poughkeepsie has her personal files locked up more tightly."

Catalina doesn't exactly strike me as the computer whiz type, Sydney thought wryly. "Does this mean you can access her e-mails?"

"What can I say? I'm on a roll!" She heard him take a celebratory sip of some presumably highly caffeinated beverage. "Hoo-boy, I think I just found what you're looking for. Wait until you get a load of this. I'm forwarding it over to you now on a secure frequency." His voice took on a more sheepish tone. "Er, I probably ought to warn you. This is strictly 'Adults Only' material."

Sydney swore she could hear him blushing over the comm-link. "I'm a big girl, Merlin. I think I can handle it."

A few seconds later the electronic file came through. Sydney opened the forwarded e-mail and found a short note addressed to Catalina, along with an attached video file. The note read:

Senora Delgado:

I have greatly enjoyed your film work,

particularly your most recent production. See attached footage for an exclusive preview.

Unless 750,000 American dollars are transferred to an account to be specified later, the same footage will be e-mailed directly to your husband.

I will be in touch shortly regarding the details of the transaction.

Enjoy the movie!

Sincerely,

A Fan

Sydney had a pretty good idea what to expect when she clicked on the attachment. The file downloaded quickly and she was immediately "treated" to several minutes of sizzling X-rated footage of a naked couple writhing on a bed, filmed from about six feet overhead. Although their flushed, ecstatic faces were occasionally obscured by their limbs and each other, there was no mistaking either Catalina or Ramon. Passionate grunts and moans emanated from the laptop's speakers, and Sydney hastily lowered the volume. The location of the sparsely furnished bedroom could not be determined from the footage itself, but Sydney suspected that she was looking at the couple's top-secret love nest in Spanish Harlem. As she rather doubted that the ambassador's wife was moonlighting in the porn industry, she also guessed that the steamy session had been recorded without the participants' knowledge, by means of a concealed camera and microphone.

No wonder Catalina looked so shocked, Sydney thought. She felt a flare of anger on the other woman's behalf. Four years ago Allison Doren had secretly taped Vaughn and Sydney making love; Sydney still remembered the pain and humiliation she had felt when she discovered the existence of the tapes. No matter what Catalina and Ramon had done, nobody deserved to have their privacy violated like this. *Nobody.*

"Pretty hardcore stuff, huh?" Marshall commented, sounding slightly embarrassed. "Insert Paris Hilton joke here."

"Or not," Sydney said. She watched the footage all the way through, resisting the urge to push the stop button, in case there was some sort of clue or message from the blackmailer. Finally the video ended, and Sydney closed the attachment. She didn't think she needed to see it again.

"Any chance you can trace the e-mail back to its source?"

"Doubtful," Marshall reported. "It came from a free e-mail account that's already been shut down. I think the blackmailer opened the account, probably from a public computer, just long enough to send this one e-mail, canceled the account, and then walked away." He sounded dismayed to be letting Sydney down. "I can poke around a bit more, but I wouldn't get your hopes up."

"Understood," Sydney said. If Marshall thought it was a long shot, then it probably couldn't be done. "Don't worry. You've already gone above and beyond the call of duty today."

She stared at the telltale e-mail and felt a stab of sympathy for Mercedes as well. Sydney's own mother had been guilty of an illicit affair (among other things), and she wondered how Mercedes would react should she ever learn the truth about her mother's indiscretions. The troubled teenager was already struggling with enough issues. The last thing she needed was another reason to resent her mother—and distrust the adults in her life.

Maybe she never has to find out, Sydney thought. She had to imagine that Catalina would be desperate to keep all this quiet, even if it meant paying off the blackmailer. But was it already too late? Apparently, Allende had a lead on the affair as well. Was he behind the blackmail, or was he just investigating the matter in his capacity as the ambassador's chief of security?

She couldn't rule out Manuel Rivera, either. Was the brash young deputy a blackmailer as well as a burglar? She had no idea how Rivera's attempt to break into the ambassador's safe could relate to Catalina's current predicament, but she doubted that the two episodes were linked solely by coincidence.

And confirmation of Catalina's affair with Ramon only gave the ambassador's wife an even stronger motive for plotting to get Delgado out of the way, perhaps by employing Niccolo Genovese or some other paid assassin. She could be both a blackmail victim *and* a femme fatale.

There was one more scenario to consider. What if Victor Delgado already knew about Catalina and Ramon, via Allende or some other source? Perhaps the ambassador was not the target of an assassination plot after all. What if Delgado had tried to hire Genovese to kill his unfaithful wife? If so, Catalina might be the one in danger.

And I thought APO was a hotbed of intrigue and double-dealing! This particular consulate made black ops look positively honest and above-board by comparison. Only Mercedes, bratty as she was, seemed innocent of any serious foul play.

Sydney hoped, for Mercedes's sake, that her mother's affair would inflict no collateral damage upon the daughter. Deep down, however, she suspected that her hopes were in vain. As Sydney knew only too well, even the best-kept secrets eventually found their way into the cold, unforgiving light of day.

And the innocent were usually the first to suffer.

I knew it, Vaughn thought sourly.

He watched the blackmail footage play out on the display screen of his cell phone. Even though the images from the streaming video were only slightly larger than a postage stamp, it was very clear what Catalina and Ramon were up to. His knuckles clenched around the wheel of the Subaru. Despite Weiss's admonitions, he couldn't help superimposing Sark's and Lauren's faces on the amorous couple in the video. Thank God he had never been forced to watch Sark and Lauren together; the scenes his imagination had conjured up were bad enough.

Never mind the time Sydney had been forced to make out with Sark while impersonating Lauren. Vaughn's blood boiled just thinking about it. He still owed Sark for that one. . . .

Vaughn had no sympathy for Catalina or her lover. They had brought their present difficulties on themselves; if the ambassador's wife hadn't chosen to cheat on her husband, then she wouldn't have made herself vulnerable to blackmail. *Serves her right,* he thought. *She made her bed, so to speak.*

Just like Lauren had.

The person he felt sorry for was Victor Delgado. How would the ambassador react to the damning footage? Vaughn could readily envision the other man's pain and anger. Anger enough to want to have Catalina killed? *Hell, yes,* Vaughn thought, remembering the intense rage he had felt against Lauren—before he gunned her down in Palermo.

He winced at the memory. If Delgado was plotting to have his wife assassinated, they needed to stop him—if only for the ambassador's sake. No man should have to live with the knowledge that he has killed his own wife.

As Jack Bristow would surely agree.

Vaughn glanced up at the curtained window across the street. Were Catalina and Ramon making love at this very moment? *Unlikely,* he thought. Chances were, they were tearing their love nest apart looking for the hidden surveillance equipment. Talk about closing the barn door after the horse had already run off—and been videotaped in flagrante to boot. No doubt they were also debating how to respond to the blackmailer's demands. Vaughn wondered how much money Catalina had socked away in her personal accounts. Enough to pay the blackmailer without her husband finding out?

"Shotgun to Merlin." Vaughn's gaze remained glued to the miniature display screen as he contacted Marshall. "Let's look into Catalina Delgado's bank accounts. See if she can manage that $750,000 on her own." He wondered how the blackmailer had arrived at that particular number. Perhaps the blackmailer was someone familiar with the Delgado family finances? "While we're at it, we should check out Rivera's and Allende's accounts as well. Find out whether either of them is having financial problems, perhaps to the tune of 750K. Look for any outstanding debts or—"

A sharp rap on the driver's side window interrupted his instructions. *Weiss is back already?* Vaughn thought, before turning his head to see Ramon standing on the sidewalk outside the Subaru, aiming the muzzle of a Colt automatic pistol at Vaughn's head. Murderous rage contorted the man's features. His black hair and clothing were soaked through, giving him an even more maniacal appearance. "Get out of the car!" he barked. "Now!"

Damn it, Vaughn thought. How had Ramon managed to get the drop on him? Even when communicating with Marshall and Sydney, he had been keeping an eye on the front door of the former tenement. Ramon must have slipped out a back door, Vaughn realized, then circled around to sneak up on the Subaru from behind. *I should have had Weiss watching the back of the building!*

"Out!" Ramon repeated. Icy rain streamed down his face, doing nothing to extinguish his apparent fury. He tugged on the locked door handle. "Keep your hands where I can see them!"

The Subaru's windows were hardly bulletproof, which left Vaughn with no choice but to comply. He swung the car door open and stepped outside onto the sidewalk. The ongoing deluge poured down on him, quickly rendering him as soggy as Ramon. Vaughn's own Beretta was tucked into the shoulder holster beneath his jacket. Vaughn doubted that the irate bodyguard would give him a chance to draw the weapon.

"Turn around. Hands on the car!" Ramon roared.

Vaughn did as he was told, turning to face the car like a suspect being picked up by the cops. It dawned on him that his comm-channel to Marshall was still open. Presumably, the attentive tech support guy was hearing all this back at headquarters. "What's your problem, man?" Vaughn protested, as though he had no idea who Ramon was. "Put that gun away. You want the car, take it!"

"Shut up, you filthy pervert!" A meaty palm slammed into Vaughn's back, shoving him into the side of the Subaru. Vaughn grunted in pain.

The muzzle of the automatic weapon jabbed into the back of Vaughn's neck, the wet metal feeling cold against his skin. Ramon frisked Vaughn with his free hand, finding the concealed Beretta. He removed the gun from its holster and tucked it into the waistband of his slacks. Spotting the cell phone in Vaughn's hand, he confiscated that as well, but missed the miniaturized comm-mike hidden beneath Vaughn's collar. Ramon poked at the keypad on the cell phone, checking its memory. *"Hijo de puta!"* he exclaimed as he spotted the X-rated footage playing on the phone's small display screen. "You stinking bastard!"

A brown station wagon came down the street. Its headlights slashed through the falling rain. Spotting the altercation, the driver slowed to see what was happening. The face of a sixty-something Hispanic man peered out the windshield.

"What are you looking at!" Ramon bellowed at the onlooker. "Get the hell out of here!"

The driver took one look at the bodyguard's enraged face—and the gun in his hand—and hit the gas. The station wagon sped away, its taillights disappearing into the distance.

Trying to avoid any more interruptions, Ramon yanked Vaughn away from the Subaru and shoved him toward the vacant lot next to the sidewalk. "Put your hands behind your head," he instructed the unarmed agent. The barrel of the Colt spurred Vaughn forward. "And don't try anything funny!"

The abandoned lot was bordered on three sides

by brick and concrete walls. At one time a wire fence had sealed off the site, but now the rusty wire lay shredded on the crumbling floor of the lot, along with miscellaneous rubble and debris. Garbage littered the uneven ground: cigarettes, soda cans, broken bottles, candy wrappers, condoms, soaked newspapers, torn magazines, and even a broken Daredevil PEZ dispenser. Brown weeds sprouted from cracks in the cement. Rainwater pooled in every depression. Distracted, Vaughn stepped in a puddle and cold water swallowed his right foot for a moment. But his freezing toes were the least of his worries.

Vaughn stumbled and splashed across the broken pavement, urged on by the relentless prodding of Ramon's gun, until they reached the wall at the rear of the lot. "Up against the wall!" Ramon ordered.

Windows opened up on the upper floors of the buildings enclosing the lot. "Mind your own business!" the gun-wielding bodyguard shouted. Most of the windows slammed shut again. Vaughn wondered if anyone would bother to call the police.

He placed his hands up against the cold, wet concrete. He couldn't help remembering the firing squad that he and Sydney had faced in North Korea a year ago. They'd gotten a last-minute reprieve on that occasion, thanks to a fortuitously placed double agent, but maybe this time his luck had run out.

"Look, Ramon," he said, dropping the bodyguard's name for Marshall's benefit. Ramon didn't seem to notice the familiarity. "Let's get out of this empty lot. Go someplace dry." He hoped Marshall was paying close attention. "Maybe we can talk about this."

"Talk?!" He grabbed Vaughn's hair and smacked his head against the wall. A jolt of pain left the APO agent momentarily dazed. "You think you're so smart with your tricky spy camera? I'll show you smart, *cabrón*!" He let go of Vaughn's hair and stepped back. "Keep your filthy hands on the wall or I'll blow your head off!"

Vaughn realized that Ramon had mistaken him for the blackmailer. "You've got this all wrong!" He glanced back over his shoulder at the furious bodyguard, looking down the barrel of the automatic. "I'm not the one who taped you and Catalina. I'm trying to find out who the real blackmailer is!"

Among other things.

"Shut your mouth, scumbag! I don't need to hear your lies." Ramon tossed Vaughn's cell phone onto the ground and crushed it beneath his heel. Fragments of plastic, metal, and crystal were ground into the rubble. "We found your spy cam, you goddamn sicko. I ought to gouge your peeping eyes from your skull!"

"I'm telling you, you've got the wrong man!"

"Bullshit!" Ramon shook his fist at Vaughn. Veins bulged at his temples. "If you didn't do it, who did?"

"I don't know!" Vaughn said honestly. He was tempted to point in Allende's direction, reveal that the security chief was also having Catalina followed, but quickly decided against it. There was too much he didn't know about what was really going on, so he was reluctant to stir the waters blindly. That could get the wrong people killed, and he already had enough deaths on his conscience. "Maybe we can help each other find the real blackmailer?"

"Yeah, right," Ramon said. His mouth twisted in a sneer. "So, who are you supposed to be, anyway? NYPD?"

"FBI," Vaughn lied. "We've been investigating reports of criminal activity at the consulate for some time now." From what Sydney had observed already, that sounded plausible enough. If the Mexican government complained, the Bureau could legitimately deny that they had anything to do with any such investigation. "Like that break-in the other night."

Ramon wasn't buying it. "That's enough! No more lies. I want to know who you're *really* working for." He spit in Vaughn's face, but the wad of saliva was practically lost amid the torrents of rain pouring down on both men. "Cough up a name—and maybe you'll walk out of El Barrio alive. *Comprende?*"

Vaughn knew Ramon was not bluffing.

As nearly as Eric Weiss could tell, the driver of the gray Chevy had not yet noticed Weiss following him. He was probably watching for Ramon or Catalina instead. Weiss darted from doorway to doorway as the unidentified man made his way down the block, occasionally glancing back over his shoulder. Once he almost caught Weiss, but the agent managed to duck behind a couple of garbage cans just in time. *That was close.*

The rain wasn't making his job any easier. Not only was he drenched, but the dismal weather had emptied the sidewalks except for him and the man with the crew cut, making it harder to remain unobserved. *Besides, this just plain sucks,* he thought as the cold water sluiced beneath his collar and down his back. Wet socks chilled his toes, and he envied Vaughn's cozy stakeout location inside the Subaru. *Next time, I get to stay in the car.*

While he waited for the man to make his next move, Weiss recalled his recent conversation with Vaughn. *I hope I wasn't out of line with that whole Lauren thing,* he worried. As a rule, he generally adopted the policy that his friend's late-and-unlamented spouse was not to be brought up, especially when Sydney was around. But he couldn't help worrying that this particular assignment might be hitting a little too close to home for Vaughn, clouding his judgment. *What kind of friend would I be if I didn't try to keep him on his game? I'm sure he'd do the same for me—if I ever married a psycho terrorist bitch!*

Satisfied that he was not being followed, the other man continued down the block until he reached the green Hyundai that Ramon and Catalina had picked up at the parking garage. The car's scratched paint job and dinged fenders gave it a distinctly pre-owned look. Weiss had to hand it to Ramon and Catalina; the unassuming vehicle was the last car you'd expect to find a movie-star-turned-ambassador's-wife in. Apparently, however, the Hyundai's state of deterioration had not been enough to fool either of the two drivers who had followed it out to East Harlem. *Nice try,* Weiss thought.

The man glanced up and down the sidewalk once more, missing Weiss behind the garbage cans, and extracted a small object from his pocket. He knelt behind the empty vehicle and placed the object underneath the car's rear bumper.

A tracer, Weiss guessed. *Not a bad idea, actually. If I get a chance, I might want to do the same thing.* Montezuma Protection Services was obviously going to some effort to keep track of Catalina Delgado's movements. *I wonder how long Allende has been keeping her under surveillance.* It occurred to him that Ramon himself worked for the consulate's security chief. *So why does Allende have his left-hand man spying on his right?*

The unidentified stranger got up and wiped his wet hands on his sopping trousers. Weiss got ready to adjust his position in case the other man started to head back his way. Instead of hiding, he might have to scurry past the guy and hope that he wasn't noticed. After all, it was a public street. . . .

But the man was not through with the Hyundai yet. Approaching the passenger's side door, he produced a set of lock-picking implements and went to work. Was he planning to steal the car, Weiss wondered, or just to plant some sort of bug inside the vehicle? Peering around the side of the trash cans, Weiss put his money on the latter scenario. Allende's man was doing just what APO would do under the same circumstances.

But to what end?

Before he had a chance to see what the man did next, an urgent voice blurted in his ear. "Merlin to Houdini," Marshall said, obviously agitated. "Shotgun is in trouble. Ramon's pulled a gun on him. They're in some sort of empty lot by the car, and Ramon's threatening to kill him!"

What the hell? Weiss thought. Spying on the Montezuma Protection employee instantly became a low priority. He ran out from behind the garbage cans, not caring if the other man saw him. He drew his gun and sprinted across the street, then ran down the sidewalk toward where they had parked the Subaru. "Hang on, pal," he muttered into his comm, hoping Vaughn was still linked to him.

Within seconds he reached the Subaru, which was empty—just as he had feared. Lifting a hand to shield his eyes from the rain, he peered into the vacant lot. The situation was just as dire as Marshall had reported. Ramon had Vaughn up against a wall, approximately fifty yards away. A gun was pointed at Vaughn's head. All Ramon needed to do was pull the trigger.

"Hey, Ramon! *Amigo!*" Weiss shouted, desperate to distract the bodyguard somehow. Gun in hand, he charged at Ramon. His heart was pounding in his chest. *"Qué pasa?"*

Ramon turned his head in confusion. His gun swung away from Vaughn, toward Weiss. Vaughn saw his opening and spun around on one leg, kicking the pistol from Ramon's hand. The gun went flying into the street, where it disappeared into a greasy puddle. Ramon reached behind his back to draw the weapon he had confiscated earlier from Vaughn, but Vaughn followed up his kick with a punch to the bodyguard's gut. Ramon staggered backward, gasping. "Hands up!" Weiss ordered. He held up a phony badge. "Freeze!"

Ramon looked from Weiss to Vaughn and back again. Realizing he was outnumbered, he bolted out of the lot. *"Vaya al diablo!"* he hollered at the two agents as he fled. *Go to the Devil!*

Weiss took aim with his gun, then lowered it. CIA policy was not to fire except when fired upon, and Weiss saw no reason to make an exception in this case. For all he knew, the fleeing bodyguard was only guilty of trying to protect Catalina from a man who was following her.

He watched helplessly as Ramon made his escape. *Screw it,* he thought, turning to check on his friend. "Are you all right, dude?"

Vaughn joined him near the front of the lot. There was a nasty bruise forming on his forehead, but otherwise he looked okay. "I feel like a drowned rat, not to mention an idiot, but that could have gone a lot worse." He slapped Weiss on the back, producing a spray of frigid droplets. "Thanks, man."

A siren wailed a few blocks away. Maybe someone had reported the confrontation in the vacant lot? "We'd better get out of here," Vaughn suggested. APO's unofficial status made encounters with the authorities problematic.

"Sounds good to me," Weiss agreed. Besides,

he couldn't wait to get into the car and start drying out. He nodded at the apartment building that had previously been the site of the ambassador's wife's sordid affair. "What about Senora Delgado?"

"Trust me," Vaughn said. "I think we've learned plenty about her today." Weiss couldn't miss the bitter edge to his friend's voice. "I'll tell you all about it on the way back."

CHAPTER 10

GRAND CENTRAL STATION
42ND STREET
MANHATTAN

The subway platform was packed with tourists and New Yorkers. Even though the early morning rush hour had been over for an hour, the underground station was filled with people. They glanced at their watches, sipped coffee, munched on bagels or breakfast bars, read their newspapers, and otherwise occupied themselves while waiting for the next train to arrive. The more impatient among them kept leaning out over the edge of the platform, hoping to spot the headlights of an oncoming train. A hanging sign promised that the uptown 4,

5, and 6 lines served this particular platform. Across two rows of parallel tracks, a similar crowd of commuters waited for the downtown trains. Rats scurried among the tracks, foraging amid the garbage littering the floor of the station.

The crowded platform was a good sign, Sydney realized. It meant that several minutes had passed since the last train had stopped at the station, so another one should be coming along soon. *I wonder if we'll manage to get seats.*

She and Mercedes were en route to the Metropolitan Museum of Art, about forty blocks north of Grand Central. Sydney hoped that a field trip would kick-start the teenager's interest in her lessons—Mercedes remained a reluctant student at best, much to Sydney's frustration.

Some tutor I'm turning out to be, she thought. *All those years of graduate work and I can't even manage to teach a class of one.*

Part of her resented having to take time off from her real mission to babysit Mercedes, but, in the long run, it was important that she maintain her cover as a concerned educator. Besides, she reminded herself, Ambassador Delgado was supposed to be busy at the UN today, attending a meeting of the Commission on Population and Development, so she wasn't likely to be missing anything at the consulate for the next few hours. The ball was in Dixon's court.

"So, there's supposed to be a good Frida Kahlo exhibit at the Met this season," she said to Mercedes. Perhaps she could get through to the girl by appealing to her Mexican heritage? "You want to check that out?"

Mercedes shrugged as though she couldn't care less. "I saw the movie," she said flatly. Her scuffed black leather jacket contrasted sharply with Syd's tan peacoat. She kept her gaze fixed on the tops of her boots. "It wasn't that great."

"Well, there are plenty of other exhibits we can visit instead," Sydney offered. "The Met has everything from ancient Egyptian artifacts to modern art and photography. You name it, they've got it: sculptures, paintings, tapestries, costumes, and so on. There's even a museum shop."

"Whatever," Mercedes muttered. "Let's just get this over with."

Syd felt like she was talking to a brick wall. She found herself envying Vaughn and Weiss, who were off keeping tabs on Mercedes's mother in hopes of learning more about the blackmail plot. At least they didn't have to deal with a blasé teenager, just the occasional gun-wielding bodyguard.

It was the day after the guys' trip to East Harlem. APO had been monitoring Catalina's e-mail account, as well as the bugs Sydney had placed around the consulate, but no progress had been made in finding out who was blackmailing the ambassador's wife, and what, if anything, her scandalous secrets had to do with those mysterious calls to Niccolo Genovese. As far as they knew, the blackmailer had not yet contacted Catalina again, nor had Carlos Allende informed the ambassador of his wife's extramarital activities. Sydney had bumped into Victor Delgado earlier that morning, as he had been heading out the door, and the personable diplomat had seemed in good spirits, not at all like a husband who had just found out his wife was sleeping with another man. Furthermore, Sydney's bugs had not recorded any nasty domestic scenes in the Delgado family's private chambers.

What is Allende waiting for? she wondered. *Is he embarrassed that Catalina's lover is a member of his own security team?* Sydney tapped her foot impatiently, and not because the train was late.

The ambassador's big speech was rapidly approaching, and she still had so many unanswered questions. *We're running out of time.*

On the other hand, Marshall had confirmed that Catalina had about $750,000 in her private bank accounts, meaning that she could pay off the blackmailer without involving her husband. Sydney wondered how Catalina's anonymous "fan" had managed to gauge her personal fortune so accurately. Maybe it was an inside job, perpetrated by someone very familiar with Catalina's affairs—in every sense of the word?

Allende? Rivera? It occurred to Syd that Ramon himself might be involved with the blackmail scheme, despite his irate confrontation with Vaughn yesterday. Had the hunky bodyguard set Catalina up? Sydney knew from personal experience just how easy it could be to lure an unsuspecting target into a compromising situation. *I do it all the time,* she thought.

A gust of cold wind blew through the tunnel, heralding the approach of an uptown train. Sydney leaned forward, craning her head to peer down the murky tunnel, and saw a pair of glowing headlights drawing nearer. A lighted green circle identified the vehicle as the 6 train, otherwise known as the Lexington Avenue Local. *That will do,* Sydney thought. The 6 wouldn't get them to the 86th Street station and the Met as quickly as an express train would, but they only had four or five stops to go anyway.

"Finally," Mercedes said bleakly.

The oncoming train revitalized the crowd on the platform. Restless commuters stirred and surged forward, encroaching upon the yellow warning line at the edge of the platform. They jostled and jockeyed for position, each hoping to be the first to enter the train—and perhaps snag a seat. Sydney stuck close to Mercedes, just in case the rebellious teen tried to give her the slip and play hooky. "If we get separated," she instructed her student, "meet me in front of the museum . . . as quickly as possible."

Air brakes squealed cacophonously, drowning out whatever snarky remark Mercedes may have muttered in reply. The train slowed to a stop. Through its windows, Sydney saw groups of passengers gathered by the car doors, waiting to exit. Grand Central was a major terminal, so she suspected a lot of people would be getting off.

Maybe we'll get seats after all?

The doors slid open and a flood of people surged from the train. The mob on the platform reluctantly gave way to let them pass, then rushed forward the moment the doorways were clear. Sydney and Mercedes let the momentum of the crowd carry them forward toward the nearest car. Sydney started thinking ahead to their day at the museum.

Is this field trip going to do any good at all, she wondered, *or am I just wasting my time?* She walked closely behind Mercedes, making sure to keep the girl in view. *If only I could get her to open up to me! Who knows? I might even learn something useful from her take on the consulate and its staff. . . .*

Suddenly, a pair of strong arms wrapped around her from behind, pinning her arms to her sides. "Don't make trouble and you won't get hurt!" a male voice barked in her ear. She felt hot breath on her neck, and whiskers scraped against her skin. The man smelled of cigarettes.

What the hell? Was this a mugging, or something more sinister?

"Hey!" Mercedes yelled indignantly, then

abruptly fell silent. Sydney saw with alarm that a second man had come up behind the girl and was hustling her toward the waiting train. Judging from Mercedes's ashen face, Sydney guessed that she had a concealed weapon pressed against her back, prodding her forward. Her unwanted companion had bloodshot eyes and a tan face badly in need of a shave, and he looked considerably larger and stronger than Mercedes. A scuffed brown duster added to his bulk.

"Move it, babe!" the thug grunted at the girl. No one else seemed to be paying the "couple" any notice. "We don't wanna keep our friends waiting."

Years of training kicked in, and Sydney threw her head back, slamming her skull into her own assailant's face. She felt his nose crumple satisfactorily. A grunt of pain sounded loudly, only inches from her ears. "Goddammit!"

His grip loosened and she tore her arms free. She kicked backward, gouging his shin with her heel. He tried to grab on to her again, but she seized his right arm with both hands and deftly flipped him over her shoulder. He landed on his back on the concrete floor of the platform with a resounding thud, barely missing two terrified commuters who dove out of the way at the last minute.

Sydney briefly looked the guy over. He sported a meticulously kept black beard, worthy of a biker or pirate, which obscured his face. *White, late twenties, yellow teeth,* she noted quickly, filing the details in her memory for later reference. *Bad breath.*

She looked for Mercedes and saw that the other thug had managed to get his captive onto the train already. For a second Mercedes's terrified eyes met Sydney's as she glanced anxiously back over her shoulder.

"Stay close!" Mercedes's attacker warned her with a menacing undertone. "I wouldn't want anything to happen to you!"

In the confusion of entering and exiting the train, no one even noticed Mercedes being abducted.

"Hang on!" Sydney called out, her cry all but lost in the din of the bustling station. "I'm coming!"

Sydney saw that the train doors were still open, and she started forward to rescue her student, but the first goon scrambled to his feet in front of her, blocking her way. "Stay out of this!" he warned her. Blood from his broken nose streamed down his face. "Her old man ain't paying you enough to interfere."

You have no idea who you're dealing with, Sydney thought grimly. Instead of backing off, she decked the guy with a roundhouse kick to his jaw. He dropped to the platform like a pile of bricks. Obviously, he'd been hired for his bulk, not his fighting skills.

But the stubborn thug had cost her precious time. Sydney's heart sank as, with a noisy hiss, the train doors slid shut, cutting her off from Mercedes and the second goon. The 6 train lurched forward, starting to pull out of the station.

"Wait! Stop!" Sydney called to the conductor, uncertain if he could hear her. She ran toward the train, waving her arms. "Stop the train!"

The train accelerated out of the station, leaving Sydney behind. She watched in anguish as the train's taillights disappeared into the subway tunnel. Within seconds it was completely out of sight.

She stopped running and stood breathlessly on the platform, wondering what to do next. Mercedes was being carried away at a rate of several blocks per minute. *I'm losing her!*

People started to emerge from behind the sheltering steel and concrete columns. A few Good Samaritans approached her apprehensively, perhaps intimidated by the brutal way she had dealt with her attacker. "Are you all right, honey?" a middle-aged black woman asked her. "Do you need anything? A doctor, maybe?"

"I'm fine, thanks," Syd said distractedly. She didn't have time to deal with any well-meaning civilians right now. How was she going to tell Mercedes's parents that their daughter had been abducted right before her eyes?

Helpful New Yorkers surrounded her. "Who were those guys?" a guy in a business suit asked her.

I have no idea, Sydney thought despairingly. She turned toward her fallen foe. The bearded guy stirred upon the platform, groaning. Blood glistened on his mustache and beard. She sprinted back to him, then kicked him savagely in the ribs. "Who are you working for?" she demanded. "Where is he taking her?"

"Screw you!" the thug said with a sneer. He spit a broken tooth onto the concrete.

Sydney kicked him again and felt a rib crack.

"Answer me!" A populated subway terminal, in front of roughly fifty witnesses, was hardly the ideal place to conduct an interrogation, but this was no time to be surreptitious. She aimed her boot at his crotch. "You do not want to mess with me!"

A flicker of fear shone in his face. Sydney knew her dad would be proud.

"Give me a break!" he pleaded. "I was just trying to make a buck!"

Another gust of wind blew through the terminal. Squealing brakes indicated that another train was pulling into the station. Sydney glanced away from her prisoner and checked the number on the front of the train.

It was the number 4. An express.

A wild idea struck her. Maybe she could still catch up with the first train after all. It would mean leaving the fallen thug behind, but it would be worth it if there was even a chance of getting Mercedes away from her abductor.

I've got to risk it!

"Excuse me, miss!" a firm voice called out. Sydney spotted a uniformed transit cop striding toward her. He scowled at the scene before him, and sounded slightly puzzled. Having no doubt received a report of a woman being attacked upon the platform, he probably hadn't expected to find

Syd torturing her assailant when he showed up. "What's going on here?"

Sydney kept one eye on the 4 train, which was letting out its passengers at this very moment. Wide-eyed commuters gawked at Sydney and her victim, no doubt wondering what they had just walked into.

"A woman has been kidnapped!" she informed the cop hurriedly, just in case her desperate plan fell through. "Mercedes Torres, of the Mexican Consulate. This man is an accomplice." A handful of frazzled passengers boarded the 4 train. "Now I've got to run."

She dashed for the nearest subway car. There was no way she was going to miss this train.

"Hey! Where do you think you're going?" the cop hollered after her. "You need to file a report!"

She raced through the open doors and onto the train. The doors whooshed shut, and Sydney caught one last glimpse of the transit cop's dumbfounded face before the express train pulled out of the station. Wasting no time, she shouldered her way through the linked subway cars until she reached the rear of the train. The final door was locked, but that only slowed Sydney for a second or two; her dad had taught her to pick more complicated locks while she was still in grade school. She eased open a sliding door and stepped out onto the small open platform outside the last car, which bucked and rattled beneath her feet as the train sped along the tracks. Sydney grabbed on to a handrail for support. The clamorous sound of the train's passage filled the tunnel.

Do I really want to try this? she asked herself, taking a second to reconsider her plan. She shucked off her winter coat to increase her mobility. The heavy peacoat fell to the floor of the platform, leaving Sydney in slacks and a green cashmere sweater. She thought of Mercedes in the kidnapper's clutches and realized she had no choice. *She was my responsibility. I can't let her down.*

Taking a deep breath to steady her nerves, Sydney climbed over the guardrail and set her feet down on the outer edge of the tiny platform. There was only an inch or two of metal to stand on, so she held on to the rail with both hands as she peered around the side of the speeding express train in search of the local train up ahead. The empty local track ran parallel to the express track, on the inside lane. Iron columns, spaced at regular intervals, rose between the two sets of tracks. Sydney had to be careful not to lean out too far. Her skull would not survive even a glancing collision with one of the sturdy metal girders.

The 4 train zipped past the 51st Street station without stopping. The 6 train had a head start on her, but the 4 was faster. To her relief, she spied the taillights of the 6. Just as she had hoped, the express train was catching up with the local.

Sydney's muscles tensed in preparation. She was only going to get one chance at this, and the timing was going to be a matter of life and death. She was going to have to jump between the iron girders at the exact moment that the two trains were running side by side, when the rear platforms on both trains were right across from each other. One wrong move, and she would end up smashed into a pillar or electrocuted by the tracks.

At least if I screw up, I won't live long enough to regret it, she thought morbidly.

She watched intently as the tail end of the 6 train grew nearer. She counted the pillars as her own train whipped past them, estimating the interval between each column. The front end of the 4 caught up with the rear of the 6, and the faster train started to pull alongside the slower. The distance between the two rear cars shrank at an alarming rate, until they were almost parallel with each other. A gap opened up between the pillars, and Sydney saw her moment. . . .

Here goes nothing.

She jumped from one train to the other, hoping that her current breath wouldn't be her last. Her legs smacked against the guardrail on the 6 train, and she tumbled headfirst onto the platform behind the rear car, hastily drawing her legs in before they could be clipped by a column. Sprawled in a heap on the cramped floor of the outer platform, it took her a second to realize that she was still in one piece.

I made it! Her heart was pounding in her chest as adrenaline coursed through her veins. Gasping in relief, she wanted to take a moment to savor her unlikely survival, but she knew that she didn't have any time to lose. Mercedes was still in danger.

Climbing to her feet, Sydney forced open the back door of the subway and rushed into the rear car. Startled faces turned in her direction, and she saw that the car was about two-thirds full. Straphangers blocked the open corridor running down the middle of the car, making it difficult to see ahead. Peering past the heads and shoulders of the commuters, she failed to spot Mercedes and her abductor. They had to be farther ahead, in one of the other cars, assuming they hadn't already exited the train.

"Coming through!" she shouted as she forced her way down the length of the car, squeezing insistently among the packed bodies of the straphangers. Dirty looks and angry protests bombarded her from all sides, but Sydney couldn't care less; all that mattered was getting to Mercedes in time. "Out of my way! Emergency!"

She raced through car after car, determined to catch up with her quarry before the train reached the next station. Clueless civilians filled the blue benches lining the interiors of the cars, while vertical steel poles gave the standing passengers something to hang on to. Advertisements were posted along the walls, above the windows. Shoving past the straphangers, it took Sydney only a few minutes to reach a car near the middle, where she found what she was looking for.

At the far end of the car, the kidnapper had Mercedes cornered against one of the side doors.

The front of his duster remained pressed against her back, concealing his weapon. Studiously minding their own business, their fellow passengers seemed oblivious to the danger facing the teenage girl, despite her tense body language and strained expression. "Only a few more stops, babe," her abductor promised, keeping his tone deceptively light.

Where is he taking her? Sydney wondered. Her best guess was that he was hoping to disappear into one of the major terminals up ahead. *Maybe 86th Street, or 125th?*

Despite her abductor's attempts to keep her quiet, Mercedes whimpered in fear. Her hands were wrapped around one of the standing metal poles. Tears glistened upon her cheeks, but no one else on the subway seemed to care; they probably just thought she was having a fight with her boyfriend.

The car door slid shut behind Sydney. All eyes turned toward the new arrival, including those of Mercedes and her kidnapper. It was hard to say who looked more shocked to see her.

"Iris!" the teenager blurted. The hope in her eyes nearly broke Sydney's heart.

"You!" the thug growled. He blinked in confusion. "How the hell . . . ?"

You wouldn't believe me if I told you, Sydney thought. "Let the girl go!" She didn't have to fake the menacing tone in her voice. "You're in enough trouble already!"

"Stay back!" he threatened her, brandishing a knife. The other passengers gasped in alarm, and backed away from the man and his hostage. "I don't know what you did to Jake, but I'm in control here!"

Wanna bet? Sydney thought. She quickly took stock of her surroundings. Out of the corner of her eye, she spotted the bright red cord of the emergency brake on the wall nearby.

Before the kidnapper could anticipate her move, she reached out and yanked hard on the brake cord, at the same time grabbing on to a handrail with her other hand and bracing her feet.

With an earsplitting squeal, the train slammed to a halt. Momentum threw Sydney forward, but she held on to the rail and managed to stay on her feet. The kidnapper, among others, wasn't so lucky. Caught off guard, he went tumbling backward, losing his grip on Mercedes, who clung to her pole.

"Mercedes, run!" Sydney shouted.

For once, the teenager did not question her. As soon as she got her balance back, she let go of the pole and sprinted toward Sydney. *"De gracias a Dios!"*

"Get behind me," Sydney told her, stepping between Mercedes and the thug. The rest of the passengers fled toward the rear of the car, desperate to escape the violent scene. Pushing and shoving, they poured into the next car. Sydney was glad to see them go. There was less chance of civilian casualties that way.

The kidnapper was already scrambling to his feet, and he looked determined to reclaim his prize. He advanced on Sydney, waving his knife before him. The serrated silver blade caught the fluorescent gleam of the overhead lighting. "You crazy bitch! Are you out of your mind? Hand the girl over . . . now!"

"Forget it," she said without hesitation, assuming a defensive stance. If his buddy back at Grand Central was any indication, this guy was just hired muscle, lacking any advanced fighting skills. She smiled at him scornfully. "Come and get her," she dared him.

He lunged at her with his knife, stabbing at her

belly. She dodged the thrust by pivoting to the left, while parrying the blow with her right arm. Then she used her left arm to block and trap the goon's own arm long enough for her to seize his knife hand and steer it away from her body. The guy grunted in frustration as she pressed her left arm against his elbow, forcing him to the floor of the car with a textbook forearm takedown. She dropped her knee onto his hyperextended arm, freeing up her left hand, and wrestled the knife from his grip.

So much for that, she thought, tucking the knife into her belt. After her death-defying leap from train to train, the brief tussle with the kidnapper was almost anticlimatic.

Facedown on the dirty tiles, the would-be attacker let loose with a torrent of obscenities. Sydney's knee kept his arm pinned to the floor, and she held on to his captured arm with both hands. Remembering Mercedes's fearful expression and tears, she was sorely tempted to break his arm, which would have been easy enough from this position, but she settled for pulling back on it painfully. The prone kidnapper yelped in agony.

Music to my ears, she thought.

"Watch your mouth!" She wanted to interrogate

him on the spot, to find out who had hired him and his buddy, but Mercedes's presence, only a few yards away, complicated matters. Sydney could hardly grill her prisoner and still maintain her cover as Iris Talbot. Explaining away her heroics since the attack at Grand Central was going to be tricky enough. Worse yet, she was going to have to turn the kidnapper over to the NYPD, not APO. *I miss the good old days,* she thought, *when I could just flash my CIA badge in an emergency.*

But she wasn't CIA anymore. At least not officially.

Making sure she still had the attacker pinned, she looked up at Mercedes. "Are you all right?" Syd asked.

"I think so," the teenager said, wiping the tears from her face. She stared at Sydney with amazement. For the first time that Syd could remember, her student actually looked her in the eyes as she spoke. "That was so . . . awesome! You saved my life!" She glanced back over her shoulder at the door Sydney had so miraculously appeared from. "I don't even know how you caught up with us, after that scuzz dragged me onto the train."

"I'll tell you all about it later," Sydney promised, making a mental note to tone down some of the more outrageous parts. "Do you have any idea who this guy is?"

Mercedes shook her head. "Never seen him before in my life."

Syd hoped Marshall could uncover the guy's rap sheet later on, as well as that of his accomplice back at Grand Central. She imagined that the transit cops already had his pal Jake in custody by now. *Who hired them, and what were they after, besides Mercedes?*

The door to the conductor's compartment slid open a crack, and a nervous-looking MTA employee peered out into the car. "Is everything under control out there? I called the authorities."

"We're good!" Sydney announced, and the conductor emerged from his booth. His turban and thick gray beard suggested that he was a Sikh. Flustered, he stared in amazement at the two women and their subdued adversary.

The train slowed, and Sydney saw that they were pulling into the 86th Street station. Uniformed transit cops patrolled the platform, waiting for Sydney to arrive on the 4 train. She guessed that the cop back at Grand Central had alerted his compatriots farther up the subway line; no doubt the transit police still wanted an explanation for that fracas on the platform. *Fine with me,* she thought. Iris Talbot would be happy to turn another thug over to the authorities.

"I don't know about you," she said to Mercedes, "but I'd like to skip the museum. I think we've had enough excitement for one morning."

The girl grinned at Sydney, revealing a surprisingly warm smile. "You think?"

How about that? Syd thought, amazed to find herself bonding with Mercedes at last. *Maybe this field trip wasn't such a waste of time after all.*

The man on the floor groaned miserably.

CHAPTER 11

MEXICAN CONSULATE

"Appalling!" Victor Delgado exclaimed. "That my own stepdaughter could be assaulted in broad daylight, right here in New York City! *Qué barbaridad!*"

The ambassador sat behind his desk, an aggrieved expression upon his face. Sydney was seated across the desk in a leather wingback chair, while Manuel Rivera and Carlos Allende stood on either side of her. Delgado had called an immediate meeting in his office to discuss the attempted kidnapping of Mercedes. The girl herself was not present; a tearful Catalina had immediately taken custody of her daughter and whisked her off to bed. For once, Mercedes had not objected to being treated like a child. Exhausted from her ordeal, she was in need of a little rest and TLC.

Thank goodness that's all she needs, Sydney thought. *Things could have turned out much worse. Who knows what that guy had in store for her.*

"I'm so sorry, Mr. Ambassador," Sydney said. She was still wearing the same clothes she had fought the attackers in, having not had a chance to change or take a shower yet. "I should have been more careful, but it all happened so quickly."

Delgado smiled sadly. "You have nothing to apologize for, Ms. Talbot. Unfortunately, such kidnappings are not uncommon in my homeland, although I had hoped that my family would be safer here in America." He heaved a heavy sigh. "In any event, my wife and I owe you our most heartfelt thanks for coming to Mercedes's rescue as you did. Your actions today were truly remarkable."

"I'll say," Rivera agreed, winking at her. "Chasing Mercedes's kidnapper through the subway system? Single-handedly overcoming not one, but two desperate criminals? That's certainly above and beyond the call of duty for a mere tutor. Are you sure you're really an English teacher and not a Navy SEAL?"

Was he joking, or was there an edge of suspicion to his tone?

Sydney tried to shrug off her martial arts prowess. "Just some tae kwan do I picked up at the Y," she said breezily. "To be honest, I can barely believe I managed to take out those two men either. At the time, I didn't think about it. I just acted on instinct."

"Some instincts!" Rivera remarked.

"Indeed," Allende added. The dour security chief eyed her dubiously. "I have known commandos who were less resourceful in a hostage situation." His words sounded less like praise than an accusation. Syd hoped that she hadn't blown her cover.

"Let's hear it for adrenaline," she said. "Guess you never know what you're capable of until an emergency hits." She made an effort to change the subject. "I'm just glad that Mercedes is okay."

"As are we all," Ambassador Delgado declared. "My family is eternally in your debt." He looked toward Allende. "I want you to tighten security here at the consulate, and assign extra protection to

Mercedes." He shook his head wearily. "She always insisted that she didn't need a bodyguard, that she could take care of herself, but I should have overruled her. This is all my fault, in a sense. I wanted to avoid another fight with my stepdaughter, so I let her have her way in this matter, even though I should have known better."

Sydney sympathized. Given his strained relationship with Mercedes, she could see why Delgado might be reluctant to impose a bodyguard on the girl despite her protests. Heck, Mercedes hadn't even wanted a tutor, let alone a full-time babysitter.

"You mustn't blame yourself, Mr. Ambassador," Rivera said smoothly. "None of us had any reason to suspect that Mercedes might be in danger."

Especially with all the blackmail and burglary going on, Sydney added silently. *Who had time to worry about a possible kidnapping, too?* She took a minute to wonder whether the attempted abduction had anything to do with the other dubious plots playing out at the consulate, including the potential assassination. She couldn't see an obvious connection, but that didn't mean it wasn't there. Maybe the drug cartels had intended to use Mercedes to stop Delgado from speaking to the UN Commission on Narcotics as an alternative to assassinating him? *In that case, I may have just forced them to go back to Plan A.*

"Of course, *claro,* security will be heightened throughout the consulate," Allende assured the ambassador. "This unfortunate incident will not be repeated. You have my word on it."

Sydney repressed a frown. Even though it was a logical precaution, the increased security was not going to make her extracurricular snooping any easier.

She wondered if Rivera felt the same way.

"*Gracias,* Carlos," Delgado said. "I have complete faith in your abilities."

Would he feel the same way, Sydney pondered, if he knew that Allende was having his wife followed? And that Catalina was having an affair with one of the very same bodyguards that Delgado now wanted assigned to his stepdaughter?

"On another front," Rivera added, "there is the little matter of Ms. Talbot leaving the scene of the initial abduction and physically assaulting two suspects." He shot Sydney a teasing smile. "Fortunately, I believe I have convinced the local authorities to overlook these technicalities in the best interests of international harmony. Especially considering the positive outcome of Ms. Talbot's actions."

The ambassador chuckled. "Well done, Manuel. The last thing we want is for Mercedes's savior to encounter any legal difficulties on account of her heroism. She should be awarded a medal instead."

"Just doing my job," she said modestly. Looking up at Rivera, she returned his smile. "Thanks for straightening everything out."

Naturally, Sloane or Hayden Chase could have made those problems go away just as easily by pulling strings behind the scenes, but letting Rivera take the credit had its advantages. The long arm of the CIA could remain safely hidden in the shadows, for one.

"No problem," he insisted, flashing his pearly white teeth. "It was the least I could do for our own resident heroine."

Delgado's face took on a more somber expression. He turned toward Allende. "Do we have any idea who these men were?"

"Not yet," Allende reported with a frown. "I have spoken with my contacts in the New York Police Department, and they inform me that the two men are local criminals of no particular distinction. Ordinary hired toughs. They claimed to have been employed by a third party, whose identity they either cannot or will not divulge." His scowl deepened and he clenched his fists at his sides. "Unfortunately, the men are American citizens, so I cannot persuade the authorities to turn over the *cabróns* for a more vigorous interrogation."

Tell me about it, Sydney thought. She hoped APO would be able to find out more about Mercedes's would-be kidnappers than Allende had. So far, she'd barely had a chance to inform headquarters of her adventure on the Lexington Avenue line. *I should contact Vaughn and the others as soon as I get back to my room. Maybe Sloane or Marshall can figure out what's going on.*

One thing was clear, however: The ambush on the subway platform had not been a random crime. The kidnappers had known exactly where she and Mercedes were going to be, and that was hardly public knowledge. Sydney had only decided on the field trip a few days before. Someone in the consulate had alerted the kidnappers to her plans.

But who?

* * *

"This is boring," Mercedes complained. Bending at the waist, she reached for the floor. "When do we get to the good stuff?"

The sixth-floor classroom had been transformed into an impromptu gym. The desks and easel had been shoved to one side to make room for several padded exercise mats. Mercedes and Sydney were dressed for a workout, with Sydney wearing a tank top, shorts, and sneakers, while Mercedes had on a black heavy-metal T-shirt and a pair of sweatpants. The teenager grunted as her outstretched fingers strained to reach the pad beneath her feet.

"Patience," Sydney advised her. Keeping her knees straight, she easily touched her toes, then extended one leg forward and repeated the stretch. "Trust me, a good warm-up routine is essential to a productive training session. You need to get your blood pumping and your muscles nice and limber."

Mercedes glanced at Sydney's well-toned physique. "Well, I guess you know what you're talking about." She straightened up and stretched her arms above her head. "This isn't exactly what I had in mind, though. You promised you were going to teach me some of those cool kung fu moves of yours."

"Don't worry. I haven't forgotten." Sydney smiled at the girl's impatience. As harrowing as their subway adventure had been, the experience had definitely broken the ice between her and Mercedes. "Just remember our deal. You'll pay more attention to your homework and lessons if I throw in a little self-defense training on the side."

"Sure thing!" the girl said excitedly. "I'm just hoping there's more to it than push-ups and splits."

Sydney glanced at her watch. They'd been exercising for about ten minutes, so she figured they had warmed up enough. "All right," she began. "First off, what I'm going to show you is no replacement for a long-term training program conducted by a qualified instructor. To truly master any form of martial arts requires a serious commitment of time and effort. All I can do is teach you a few basic tricks."

"Got it," Mercedes said. "You can skip the disclaimers. I'm not expecting you to turn me into a black belt by Tuesday. Let's cut to the chase."

"Okay," Sydney said. "Just remember that I've

been practicing some of these moves since I was nineteen, and that was, well, more years back than I want to admit." Her mind flashed back to those early days, right after she had first been recruited by SD-6, when she had often sparred in the gym with her first partner and love, Noah Hicks. A pang went through her heart as she recalled her final battle with Hicks in a kitchen in Australia. She hoped Mercedes would never know the pain of having to kill an old boyfriend in self-defense. "So you want to make sure you know what you're doing before you take on an army single-handedly. When in doubt, it's almost always safer to run than fight."

"Yeah, I can see that," Mercedes said. "But what if I get attacked on the subway next weekend? What am I supposed to do?"

"Besides letting your bodyguard handle it?" Sydney wondered just how much fear the kidnapping attempt had put into Mercedes. Beneath her cocky attitude, was she genuinely frightened of being attacked again? Perhaps this insistence on learning some self-defense moves was the teenager's way of trying to regain a sense of security. "I suppose I can see why you might like to have a few options of your own."

"Exactly!" Mercedes exclaimed. "Now we're getting somewhere."

Sydney decided to start off with some basics. "Okay. There are a lot of good fighting systems out there, but the one I know the best is called Krav Maga. It's a hand-to-hand combat system developed by the Israeli military that emphasizes practical, real-world situations as opposed to tournament competitions. The idea is to blend offensive and defensive moves into seamless combinations of strikes and blocks. There's a whole repertoire of releases and counterstrikes you can learn, but let's begin with a scenario like we ran into on the subway the other day."

She stepped out into the middle of the exercise mats and beckoned for Mercedes to join her. "I'm going to demonstrate one simple escape technique. Now, ideally, you want to practice these moves until you don't even have to think about them anymore. You want to train your mind and body to react instinctively, so that one movement flows swiftly into another without hesitation, what the Israelis call *retzev.*" She went through a quick combination of kicks and punches to show what she meant. "We're going to do this one step at a time, though, in slow motion so nobody gets hurt."

"Not getting hurt is good," Mercedes granted. "I can appreciate that."

Sydney was amazed at how much more cooperative the girl had become since Sydney had decked her abductor on the 6 train. She positioned herself in front of Mercedes, with her back to her student. "Okay, we're going to pretend that you're attacking me."

"Ooh!" Mercedes enthused. "I've waited my whole life for a teacher to say that to me!"

"Don't get carried away," Sydney said, glad to discover that the girl apparently had a sense of humor as well. "Now lock your forearms around my neck like this." She showed Mercedes how to use both arms to lock Sydney in a chokehold, with her hands clasped together securely. "This is a particularly nasty hold because the attacker can easily crush your windpipe or cut off the flow of blood to your brain. It's a strangulation move, but there are ways to get out of it. You can try a backward head butt, like I did to that guy who grabbed me on the subway platform, or, if that doesn't work, you can try a slightly trickier move."

Ducking her chin, she turned her head toward

the juncture of Mercedes's hands. "You always want to turn toward the side where the bad guy's hands are clasped, which is the way out, and not toward his elbow, which you're not going to be able to tear apart unless you're the Incredible Hulk." At the same time, she reached up and grabbed on to Mercedes's forearm with both hands. "Now take hold of the arm right below your chin, as close as possible to where the attacker's hands are locked together, and pull it away from your neck."

She demonstrated what she meant, forcefully yanking Mercedes's arms downward and away from her neck. "Now, as soon as you get a little breathing room, you turn your shoulder into his, then step backward and under your attacker's armpit while holding his arms tightly against your body." Her hair brushed against the girl's side as her motion caused Mercedes to bend forward at the waist. Sydney's rear leg shot up toward the teenager's midsection. "Bingo! I just kneed you in the gut."

She let go of Mercedes's arms and took a step away from her student. "At this point, if we were fighting for real, I'd be kicking and punching you continuously in true *retzev* fashion. And you'd be on the losing end of the fight."

"Wow!" the teenager exclaimed. "That is so cool!"

Nice of you to think so, Sydney thought. "Did you follow all that?"

"I think so," Mercedes said. Sydney could see the girl trying to reconstruct the steps in her mind.

"We'll see about that." She circled around Mercedes until she was right behind her student. "Let's try it again, but this time switching places so that I'm attacking you." She stepped forward and gently locked her forearms around the girl's neck. "You ready?"

"Bring it on!" Mercedes challenged her.

Sydney grinned at the girl's enthusiasm. *If only I can get her to devote a fraction of this concentration to the rest of her studies!* Still, at least she was finally connecting with Mercedes. And hopefully these training sessions would help restore the teenager's confidence after what she went through on the subway the other day. *It can't hurt to teach Mercedes how to defend herself,* she thought. *Especially with all the danger and intrigue surrounding the consulate these days.*

CHAPTER 12

BOOKSTORE 5TH AVENUE MANHATTAN

It was seven o'clock on a Saturday night, and the five-story bookstore on Fifth Avenue was full of shoppers. Ray Charles played over the stereo system as customers browsed the bookshelves and magazine racks, or relaxed at the café located on the ground floor. Sydney sat alone at one of the café tables, sipping hot chai from a paper cup. A partially nibbled blueberry scone rested on a glass plate in front of her as she flipped through the latest issue of the *New Yorker*. A new coat, replacing the tan one she left on the express train, was draped over the back of her chair. Although she appeared to be engrossed in her magazine, she was actually scanning her surroundings to make sure she was really alone.

She wished she were back at the consulate, monitoring the situation there, but Iris Talbot would probably enjoy a night out, so Sydney had felt obliged to act accordingly and leave the brownstone in order to maintain her cover. The bookstore seemed like a plausible venue. Where else would a bookish young English instructor go to unwind? If anyone was following her, they would find nothing suspicious about her destination.

Too bad I can't get together with Vaughn tonight. She missed his comforting presence. But that would be even riskier than before, now that Ramon had seen Vaughn's face. And she couldn't afford to take any chances, not after that incident on the subway. She still wasn't sure whether Rivera and Allende had bought her flimsy explanation for why she had suddenly turned into an action movie heroine. *Lord knows I wouldn't believe it.*

She discreetly checked out the other patrons in the café. There were about eight other customers nearby, but no one appeared to be paying much attention to her.

Just another night at the bookstore, Sydney thought. As far as she knew, she wasn't under surveillance by Allende or anyone else, and nothing around her was setting off any warning signals in her mind. After so many years in the field, she liked to think that she knew when she was being covertly observed, and she didn't appear to be the subject of surveillance right now. *Looks like the coast is clear.*

She glanced around one more time to confirm that nobody was eavesdropping, then dialed a special, unlisted number on her cell phone. Her comms would have worked just as well, but the phone was less conspicuous. If someone was spying on her, she didn't want to be seen conversing with empty air.

"Hi! Iris here. What do you have for me?"

"Howdy!" Marshall greeted her from three thousand miles away. It was 4 P.M. in L.A. "You know, I've got a second-cousin named Iris, up in Juneau, Alaska. . . ." He caught himself digressing and cut to the chase. "Anyway, I've got some fresh intel for you, some of it intriguing. First off, I'm afraid we struck out where those two guys on the subway are concerned. We couldn't find any connection between them and any of the principals in your case, including the late Niccolo Genovese. They're a couple of low-life hoods who have probably never even heard of Genovese, or Montezuma Protection Services for that matter."

Just like Allende reported, Sydney acknowledged. The subway kidnappers were starting to look like a dead end, even though she remained convinced that the attempted abduction was somehow connected to the other dubious goings-on at the Mexican Consulate. "What else do you have?"

"Glad you asked." Marshall's voice assumed a more eager tone. "We've been looking into Manuel Rivera, like you suggested, and guess what? He doesn't exist."

Sydney nearly choked on her chai. "What do you mean?"

"It turns out there is no such person as Manuel Rivera, at least not the one presently employed by the Mexican Consulate, just an impressively fabricated paper trail worthy of . . . well, us." A note of grudging admiration could be heard in the tech guy's voice, as well as a degree of apprehension. "You'd better watch yourself, Iris. Whoever Rivera is, he's got some high-level intelligence connections."

"Point taken," Sydney said, as she absorbed this latest development. "Is this something the big drug cartels would be capable of pulling off?"

"Maybe," Marshall answered uncertainly. "It's not exactly their style, but they've got money to burn and there are a lot of unemployed spooks out there, especially now that the Alliance and K-Directorate have been shut down.

But they're not the only ones, Sydney reminded herself. She once again recalled the suave young deputy attempting to break into Ambassador Delgado's hidden safe. She still didn't know what he had been looking for, let alone why someone had gone to so much trouble to place him in the consulate under a phony name. Rivera had known about the proposed field trip to the Met, she remembered, and he could conceivably have found out about Catalina and Ramon as well. As the ambassador's right-hand man, he was certainly in a position to orchestrate both the kidnapping and the blackmail schemes. And his apparent background in intelligence put him in the same circles as a world-class assassin like Genovese.

"Thanks, Merlin!" she said to Marshall. "You've given me a lot to think about."

All at once, “Manuel Rivera” shot to the top of her list of suspects. *Who are you, really?* she wondered. *And what exactly are you after?*

“You’re back early,” the guard in the foyer commented as Sydney returned to the consulate a little after eight. She signed in at the front desk. “Aren’t you sick of this place yet?”

“Guess I’m more wiped out than I realized.” She lifted her arm so he could see the shopping bag she had brought home from the bookstore dangling from her wrist. “Think I’ll just settle in with a good book.”

In truth, after receiving Marshall’s news about Rivera, she had found it hard to concentrate on her phony night out. After finishing her chai and scone, she had browsed restlessly among the bookshelves before deciding that she had goofed off enough to satisfy any lurking shadows. She had picked up the new John Irving novel to add an extra touch of verisimilitude to her cover, then headed back to the consulate to figure out what her next move should be. Somehow she needed to unravel Rivera’s alias without exposing her own.

Easier said than done, she thought.

The guard sighed as though he thought there were better ways a pretty young woman could be spending her evening, then glanced perfunctorily at her security pass. The ritual was part of the new security crackdown that had been instituted at the consulate ever since the kidnapping attempt. "You're cool," he pronounced. "Enjoy your book."

"Thanks!" Sydney said.

As she climbed the stairs to her room, she noted that the consulate was unusually quiet. Aside from the security guards, most of the staff had left for the evening, while Ambassador Delgado and his wife, Sydney recalled, were attending a fund-raiser at Lincoln Center, under the watchful eyes of agents Vaughn and Weiss. Even Mercedes had been allowed to go out to the movies with a friend, albeit with an armed bodyguard in tow. *This might be a good time to do another search of Delgado's office,* Sydney thought. She decided to drop her bags off in her room and then see whether anyone was working late on the third floor. *Maybe I should clear the search with headquarters first?* she wondered.

Arriving at the top of the stairs, she headed down the hall toward her room, where she automatically checked the thin strip of transparent tape she had sealed the door with before leaving. She froze when she saw that the tape had been torn in two.

Someone had been in her room.

Were they still there? She tiptoed up to the door without making a sound. Pressing her ear against the door, she listened carefully. Her eyes widened as, through the wood, she heard somebody moving about in her private quarters.

She reminded herself that she had left nothing incriminating for the intruder to find. Even the hard drive of her laptop was filled with bogus documents and e-mails supporting her alias, with her real files carefully encrypted and hidden among multiple drafts of a thesis paper titled "False Reflections: Comparing the Use of Mirror Images in the Works of Mark Twain and Fyodor Dostoevsky." Sydney was perversely proud of the paper, which contained enough impenetrable academic jargon to discourage all but the most masochistic of snoops. She dared anyone to read it to the end.

In any case, the fact that anyone was combing her room at all was disturbing, since it meant that someone already suspected Iris Talbot of being more than a mere tutor.

Trying the doorknob, she found that it was locked from the inside. She stepped back and fished the key from her purse, then quietly inserted it into the lock. For what seemed like the hundredth time this mission, she wished that English tutors routinely carried guns. *All right, let's see who's in there.* She turned the key until the lock clicked softly, then barged into the room without warning.

Manuel Rivera looked up in surprise.

The slick young deputy had been searching through Sydney's closet when she caught him in the act. He jumped backward as though electrified, yanking his hands away from the clothes hanging in the closet. Sydney noticed with relief that his hands were empty. It appeared that they were both unarmed.

"Ms. Talbot!" he blurted out. He backed away from her, momentarily at a loss for words. He slicked back his hair with his hand and struggled to regain his composure. "I was just looking for you."

"Sure you were!" Sydney said harshly. She realized at once that she could hardly call for security, not without raising the whole question of why anyone would want to search her room in the first place. She closed the door behind her, fully prepared to confront Rivera on her own. "What the hell are you doing in my room?"

His eyes narrowed as he watched her shut and lock the door. He must have realized that she didn't want to deal with Allende's men any more than he did, for when he spoke again he sounded considerably less alarmed. "I have my reasons," he said with a smirk. "Let's just leave it at that."

He took a step toward the door, but Sydney held out her arm to stop him. "Sorry, Manuel. That's not going to cut it." She looked him squarely in the eye with the same steely gaze with which she had faced down some of the world's most dangerous terrorists. "You're not leaving until I find out what is going on!"

"Try and stop me," he said. Marching forward, he tried to push his way past her arm, only to have Sydney sweep her leg around his and deliver a palm-heel strike to his chest. Her shin collided with the back of his knee and he went tumbling backward, landing flat on his back on the floor.

"All right," she said. "How's that for a start?"

He stared at her incredulously, momentarily taken aback by what had just happened. Then a smirk appeared on his face and he eyed her with a certain wolfish anticipation. "So that's how you want to play it," he said with a leer. He sprang back onto his feet and raised his fists in front of him. "Okay, then. Let's dance, senorita!"

Sydney assumed a defensive stance of her own. He came at her with his right fist drawn back to deliver a knockout punch. *Like I'm going to let him get that close,* she thought disdainfully. She threw a roundhouse kick at the oncoming deputy, but, to her surprise, he sidestepped at the last minute and caught her leg between his left arm and his body, leaving her balancing on one foot. Before she could even try to extricate her leg from his trap, he grabbed on to the captured limb with both hands and spun her to the right, letting go at just the right second to send her flying across the room. Unable to halt her momentum, she plowed into the end table next to the bed. A reading lamp crashed to the floor, the lightbulb inside popping in a burst of sparks that left blue spots dancing in front of Sydney's eyes.

Damn! she thought. *He's a better fighter than he is a snoop.*

Blinking to clear her watery eyes, she saw Rivera heading for the door once more. She reached out for something to throw at him, and her fingers found an empty water glass that had been sitting on the end table, now lying next to a soggy patch of carpet. She hurled the glass at the door and it shattered on impact, an explosion of broken shards driving Rivera backward away from the door.

She jumped to her feet as he staggered past her. A side kick to his ribs knocked him across the room, and he swore loudly as he smacked his hip against the edge of Sydney's desk. "You know," he accused her, "you don't fight like a schoolteacher."

"You just haven't gone to the right schools," she replied.

Determined to stay on the offensive, she crossed the distance between them and kicked out at his back, hoping to nail a kidney. A wooden chair was nestled against the desk, however, and Rivera grabbed the back of the chair and swung it like a club at the female agent. Cheap wood splintered loudly against her side, and Sydney was sent reeling toward the window, where the white cotton curtains were drawn. The curtains entangled her, wrapping about her like a shroud, and she experienced a suffocating moment of claustrophobia.

Rivera slammed into her from behind, smashing her face and chest into the glass. The glass didn't crack, but she felt like she'd been smacked across the face with a two-by-four. She heard fabric rip as the curtains tore away from the rod above the window, giving her just enough slack to drive her elbow upward into Rivera's jaw. It connected with a satisfying *crack.*

Grunting in pain, he staggered backward a few inches. Sydney worked a leg free and kicked out blindly behind her. To her disappointment, she missed Rivera's crotch, but rammed her heel into his thigh, forcing him to retreat farther. She heard him limp away.

That's better, she thought. Seizing cotton fabric by the handful, she tore the last of the curtains away from her and stepped away from the crumpled folds on the floor. She spun around to look for Rivera, but he found her first. His hand sank into her long brown hair and yanked her head back savagely. Sydney bit down on her lip to keep from crying out as he made a tight fist above her scalp, tugging on her hair by its roots in an attempt to keep her off balance.

Fortunately, she knew just how to defend herself against such an attack, thanks to her Krav Maga training. Instead of pulling away from the pressure being exerted on her scalp, which would only tear her hair out and increase the pain, she moved toward Rivera, pivoting 180 degrees until they were face to face. She jabbed her fingers into his throat, and he made a gagging sound before letting go of her hair and stepping away.

But Sydney didn't let up. They were fighting in close quarters now, so she hit him with a left hook to his jaw. He threw a straight punch at her head, but she ducked beneath the blow and administered a sharp jab to his gut. He doubled over in agony, clutching his stomach, and she rose up to deliver a downward elbow strike between his shoulder blades.

That should do the trick, she thought.

Sure enough, he dropped face-first onto the floor, gasping for breath. Sydney knelt down on top of him, digging her knee into the small of his back. She pressed down on his neck with her forearm. "Now are you ready to tell me what you were looking for?"

But before he could breathe a word, a sudden rap at the door interrupted her interrogation of the prostrate deputy. "Ms. Talbot! What's happening in there?" The stern voice of Carlos Allende came through the door. The doorknob rattled violently. "Open up at once!"

Not now! Sydney thought. The noisy fight had obviously attracted the attention of security. She exchanged an anxious glance with Rivera, who looked just as worried as she was by the security chief's unwanted arrival. Like her, he had no desire to reveal his secrets to Allende and his men. *We can settle our differences later,* she decided. *Right now we have a bigger problem.*

"The door, Ms. Talbot!" Allende barked loudly. It was an order, not a request. "Open up this minute, or I will have the door knocked down." A shoulder slammed against the wooden door from the other side. "We're coming in!"

"Just a minute!" Sydney called back desperately. She glanced around the room, which had been destroyed by the no-holds-barred brawl. Broken glass littered the floor, and the overturned lamp lay shattered by the bed. The chair was in two pieces and the torn curtains lay in a heap in front of the door to the balcony. How in the world was she going to explain all this wreckage to Allende?

There was only one option.

"Get into the bed!" she hissed at Rivera. She removed her knee from his back and rolled off of him so that he could scramble to his feet. Peeling off her sweater and jeans, she stripped down to her underwear and tossed her clothes onto the floor. Following her lead, Rivera hastily pulled off his shirt and jacket as he dived beneath the covers of Sydney's bed.

"Ms. Talbot!" The door shuddered as the guard delivered another blow, its hinges pulling away from the wall. "Answer me, senorita!"

"One more second!" Sydney pleaded. She ran to her closet, the same one that Rivera had been rifling through several minutes ago, and yanked a terrycloth robe from its hanger. "I'm not decent!" Throwing the robe over her seminakedness, she dashed to the door, unlocked it, and tugged it open. "Here I am," she gasped breathlessly. Sweat gleamed on her face, and her light brown hair was completely disheveled. "Sorry to keep you waiting."

Carlos Allende, as well as at least half a dozen guards, stood outside her door. Sydney was surprised to find Allende himself present at this time of night; apparently, he was taking his mandate to overhaul the security at the consulate very seriously.

Just my luck, she thought.

The security chief's eyes were alight with anger. His scarred face was cross and unforgiving. "This is a serious matter, senorita!" he upbraided her. "I have reports of a violent disturbance in your room!"

"Violent?" Sydney repeated in mock surprise. Her robe fell open and, blushing, she tugged it closed again. "Um, this is kind of embarrassing, but I'm afraid there's been a bit of a misunderstanding." She leaned toward Allende and lowered her voice, as if trying to avoid being overheard by his men. "I'm not exactly alone in here, if you know what I mean. I have . . . company. Of the male variety."

A few of the guards could not resist snickering. Allende silenced them with an icy glance, then turned back toward Sydney. His face held no sympathy for her, nor did it betray any inclination to spare her feelings. "I'm afraid I must see for myself, Ms. Talbot."

Sydney cringed. "I was afraid of that." She stepped aside to let Allende enter, then closed the door before his men could follow him. Broken glass crunched beneath his boots.

Allende's eyes widened at the sight of Manuel Rivera, naked from the waist up, occupying Sydney's bed. Rumpled sheets covered the lower part of his body, leaving Allende free to imagine the worst. Like Sydney, Rivera was sweaty and disheveled, lending support to the scenario that they were trying to act out. His hair was a mess, and he was flushed from his exertions. "Carlos," Rivera said sheepishly. "My apologies for disturbing your evening." He winked at Allende. "Believe me, that was not my intention!"

Sydney felt like slapping him across the face.

"I see," Allende said hesitantly. Looking away from the man in the bed, he scanned the rest of the room. Allende seemed somewhat taken aback by the extent of the disorder. "You and Ms. Talbot did . . . all this?" he asked incredulously.

Sydney blushed again. "I guess we got a little carried away."

"So it appears," Allende said severely. His opinion of American schoolteachers seemed to be plunging by the second.

I can live with that, she thought.

"Please," she entreated him, tying her robe shut, "don't tell the ambassador and Senora Delgado about this. My job and my reputation are at stake."

"Perhaps you should have thought of that earlier," he scolded her, "before throwing the entire building into an uproar."

Rivera took a more conciliatory tone. "Carlos, surely we can overlook this one little . . . indiscretion?" He gave Allende another conspiratorial wink, implying that they were both men of the world. "After all, Ms. Talbot did save Mercedes from those filthy *cabróns* the other day. The ambassador himself said that his family owed Iris an enormous debt."

"Well . . . I suppose Ms. Talbot deserves some special consideration after her recent ordeal." He grudgingly turned toward the door, apparently satisfied that the security of the consulate had not been compromised. "I cannot guarantee that my men will not pass on gossip, but I shall keep this incident out of my report."

"Oh, thank you so much!" Sydney gushed. "I'm so sorry for all the confusion."

Allende gave them both one last scowl as he left the room. "Next time, get a hotel room."

Like there's going to be a next time, Sydney thought wryly. *Or a first time, for that matter.* She kept one eye on Rivera as she listened to Allende and his men depart. Breathing a sigh of relief, she turned back toward her opponent. She assumed a defensive stance, her hands raised in front of her.

Now that the crisis was over, she blamed Rivera for putting her in such an awkward position in the first place. *What if Mercedes hears about this?* she wondered with regret, even though she knew she had bigger things to worry about. *What kind of role model does that make me?*

She glared at the man in her bed, who seemed in no hurry to get out of it.

"So, are you ready to talk yet?"

"I don't know," Rivera replied, reclining against the headboard. To her annoyance, he appeared to be enjoying the situation. "Shall we pick up where we left off, or do we need to get that hotel room?"

You wish, she thought. She snatched up his shirt from the floor, wadded it up into a ball, and hurled it at his head. "I have a better idea," she stated coolly. "How about we lay our cards on the table? You first."

This was a risky ploy, but Sydney decided to go with it. At this point, her cover was pretty much blown anyway, at least as far as Rivera was concerned. Besides, she could hardly beat the truth out of him with Allende right downstairs.

"Why me?" he challenged her.

"You're the one who got caught breaking and entering," she pointed out. "And not for the first time. I know it was you who set off the burglar alarm when you tried to break into the ambassador's safe. And I know your real name isn't Manuel Rivera."

Her confident assertions wiped the smirk from his face. He considered his options as he pulled his shirt back on. He threw back the sheets and swung his feet over the edge of the bed, so that he faced Sydney from a sitting position. She made a mental note to wash her bedding.

"Very well," he said finally. "My real name is not important. What matters is that I work for CISEN, the Mexican intelligence agency. We've been investigating the ambassador for some time."

CISEN? Sydney had worked with their operatives before, back during her CIA days. "Investigating Ambassador Delgado? Why is that?"

The man who called himself Manuel Rivera scowled. "Victor Delgado is not nearly as squeaky-clean as he would like everyone to believe. We have reason to suspect that he has diverted government funds into his accounts, and that he has some deeply buried links to organized crime." Rivera winced as he massaged his battered jaw. "I was hoping to find evidence of his illegal activities in his safe, but the mechanism was more sophisticated than I had anticipated."

Or you're just a lousy safecracker, Sydney thought. She was disappointed to hear that Delgado might be crooked, but she knew better than to dismiss Rivera's accusations out of hand. Life had taught her never to take anything at face value. "What about Delgado's anticorruption crusade, and his campaign against drug trafficking?"

"Window dressing and misdirection," Rivera replied. "To divert suspicion from himself and promote his reputation as a reformer."

Sydney had to admit that she had heard less plausible stories. For example, according to Dixon, Sloane was in town to receive some sort of UN award for his work with Omnifam. *If Arvin Sloane can be honored as a humanitarian,* she thought, *then why can't Victor Delgado's upright persona be a fraud as well?*

"How do I know you're telling the truth?" she asked Rivera.

"You don't," he answered honestly. "Later on, after I know more about your own agenda, I might be willing to show you some of my files, but there's nothing conclusive—unless perhaps you know something I don't." He gazed at her expectantly. "Your turn."

"Not so fast," she said. "What about your real name? I'm going to need that to verify your credentials with CISEN."

"Fine," he answered archly. "As long as you're willing to tell me your real name in return."

Sydney hesitated. She guarded her true name zealously, in order to preserve some vestige of a personal life. No way was she going to give an operative of uncertain loyalties the ability to track down Sydney Bristow. Too many of her old enemies knew where to find her already.

"That's not going to happen," she admitted.

Rivera nodded knowingly. "I thought as much. Despite our scandalous behavior, I don't think we're quite on a first-name basis yet." He tried smoothing his hair back into place. "I've told you why I'm here. Now I want to know what kind of English teacher fights like an Israeli commando and knows far more than she should."

"I'm CIA," she lied, sort of. If necessary, the Agency could deny any connection to her, paint her as a former agent gone rogue. "I'm investigating a possible assassination plot against Ambassador

Delgado." She filled him in on the Genovese connection, omitting APO's involvement, and brought him up to speed on the blackmail scheme as well. The latter had clearly flown under his radar.

"Catalina and Ramon?" He arched an eyebrow. "I've occasionally suspected as much, but I had no idea she was being blackmailed."

"And you have no idea who might have videotaped them together?" she pressed. "Or arranged to have Mercedes abducted?"

He shook his head. "Not a clue, I'm afraid. That came as a complete shock to me as well. And this is the first I've heard of Niccolo Genovese." He sounded genuinely concerned by what Syd had told him. "Are you sure that the ambassador was intended to be Genovese's target? What if Delgado was the one who was in contact with this killer?"

"Always a possibility," she conceded, especially if the Mexican agent's accusations were true and Delgado was a dirty politician. In which case, there were any number of people whom Delgado might want dead: Catalina, his unfaithful wife; Ramon, his wife's lover; Rivera, the spy in his office.

And what about Mercedes? she thought, as a troubling thought occurred to her. For the first time, she entertained the possibility that the ambassador himself might have had something to do with the teenager's near-kidnapping. Sydney remembered the conspicuous absence of any photos of Mercedes in Delgado's office. Certainly, there seemed to be no love lost between Victor Delgado and his embarrassment of a stepdaughter. But would he actually go so far as to have her killed?

Please, no. Not Mercedes.

CHAPTER 13

ALOHA DINER
23RD STREET
MANHATTAN

The lunch rush was over, so there were plenty of empty booths and tables at the popular Greek diner. Still, the old man preferred to sit at the counter near the front of the restaurant, sipping noisily on spoonfuls from a large bowl of chicken noodle soup. A worn Army surplus jacket was draped over his body, and a fraying red scarf was wrapped around his neck. Thin white hair covered his scalp. A tinted visor protected his eyesight from the glare of the overhead lights, and fingerless gloves kept his hands warm. His wizened features put his age at seventy or older. A gnarled wooden cane was propped up against his stool.

"Anything else I can get for you, old-timer?" the waiter behind the counter asked.

"Maybe some more crackers?" the elderly customer replied. He had a hoarse, quavery voice that hinted at a lifetime of tobacco abuse. "And a refill on my water?"

"No problem," the waiter said. He tossed a handful of Saltines onto the counter in front of the old man. "I'll be right back with that water."

"Thanks, sonny!"

Michael Vaughn watched the waiter stroll away from him. His face itched, and he resisted the urge to scratch at the latex prosthetics glued to his skin. The heavy disguise was a pain, but there had been no way around it. Ramon had already seen his real face. The makeup also served to cover the ugly purple bruise on his forehead, left over from when the hot-tempered bodyguard had slammed Vaughn's face into that wall up in Spanish Harlem.

He raised a napkin to his lips, hiding his mouth. "Shotgun to Houdini. How you doing out there?" he whispered into his comm.

"I'm freezing, if you must know!" Weiss

replied. The other agent was stationed right outside the diner, disguised as a homeless panhandler. The last time Vaughn had seen his buddy, before stepping inside the restaurant, Weiss had been squatting against the wall of the comic book shop next door. A ratty-looking pink comforter had been pulled over his head like a tent and a battered cowboy hat further concealed his dark hair, while an olive green scarf covered his face from the nose down. A disposable paper cup sat on the sidewalk in front of him, collecting spare change from passersby. A hand-lettered cardboard sign leaning against the wall beside the apparent vagrant read PLEASE HELP! GOD BLESS YOU!

"Next time, you get to play the homeless dude," Weiss griped. "I don't think this outfit has been washed since the Cuban Missile Crisis. I smell like a sewer!"

"The price of authenticity," Vaughn commented philosophically. He smiled at his friend's vociferousness. "You know what they say: God is in the details."

Weiss snorted into his comm. "Easy for you to say! Thank God Nadia is still on assignment in Italy. One whiff of me like this, and any chance of going on another date with her would go right down the toilet."

"I'm sure Nadia understands the demands of undercover work," Vaughn assured him, even as he wondered how Jack and Nadia were faring in Europe. Last he had heard, they had arranged a meeting with Niccolo Genovese's elusive associate, The Smoke. Vaughn wished the other agents luck. Despite Sydney's efforts at the consulate, it felt like they were no closer to finding out Genovese's connection to Ambassador Delgado or his staff. Perhaps Jack and Nadia could persuade The Smoke to shed some light on the mystery. *If anyone can get someone to talk,* Vaughn thought, *it's Sydney's dad.* The elder Bristow's brutal interrogation techniques had been known to shock even his fellow agents.

Not that Sydney hadn't made some progress in untangling the myriad webs of deceit at the Mexican Consulate. At least they knew about Manuel Rivera now, assuming his story checked out. The CIA, in the person of Hayden Chase, was trying to confirm with CISEN that they had an agent placed in the Mexican Consulate in New York.

"Hey, buddy. Pass the ketchup?"

A thick Brooklyn accent came from farther down the counter, a few seats away from Vaughn, where a male Caucasian wearing a windbreaker and a Yankees cap was enjoying a cheeseburger and fries. The man was one of the few customers patronizing the diner at the moment. He nodded at the bottle of Heinz sitting on the counter a few inches away from Vaughn's bowl of soup.

"Be my guest." He slid the bottle down to his neighbor, who proceeded to drown his fries in ketchup. Vaughn went back to his soup.

Weiss spoke to him in his ear. "Heads up, pal. Here come Romeo and Juliet."

The door to the diner swung open, admitting a cold breeze as Ramon and Catalina entered. *More like Lady Chatterly and her lover,* Vaughn thought acerbically. *Juliet wasn't already married when she took up with Romeo.*

Vaughn had been anticipating the couple's arrival. By monitoring Catalina's e-mails, not to mention the bugs Sydney had placed around the consulate, APO had learned that Catalina had agreed to pay off the blackmailer, and that the transaction was scheduled to take place at the diner any minute now. He and Weiss were on hand to observe the event, even though, as of yet, no definite link had been established between the blackmail and the potential assassination. Vaughn was curious to see who showed up to handle the exchange.

Bent over his soup bowl, he cautiously avoided staring at Ramon and Catalina as they walked by him. Miniature LCD screens inside his visor allowed Vaughn to watch them indirectly. For once, the ambassador's adulterous wife was not dressed to kill; she wore a shapeless gray overcoat that seemed deliberately chosen for its drab and nondescript qualities, and her face was drawn and taut behind designer sunglasses. She clung to Ramon for support, while the bodyguard carried a laptop computer under his arm. His own face was sullen and unsmiling.

They took a seat at a booth at the rear of the diner, several yards away from the counter. A waiter wandered over to take their order, even though neither of the pair looked particularly hungry. Catalina squirmed restlessly. Ramon was visibly seething as he opened the laptop and set it up on the table before them. They watched the front entrance avidly, with both apprehension (Catalina) and barely checked anger (Ramon).

Vaughn had no sympathy for either of them.

"Oops!" He "accidentally" knocked over his cane. Leaning over to recover it from the floor, he subtly adjusted its position so that it was aimed at the rear booth. The parabolic microphone hidden inside the faux wooden walking stick transmitted the couple's conversation directly into Vaughn's earpiece.

"Where the hell is this guy?" Ramon snarled, glancing impatiently at his watch. "He's supposed to be here by now!"

"Please, Ramon!" Catalina pleaded. "Don't lose your temper. You promised you wouldn't make a scene." She dabbed at her eyes with a silk handkerchief. "I just want this all to be over!"

You should have thought of that before you cheated on your husband, Vaughn thought. Behind his visor his eyes were cold and unforgiving.

Weiss's voice broke into the transmission from the booth. "Looks like it's showtime," he alerted Vaughn. "And take a gander at who's dropping by!"

Vaughn glanced toward the door as a familiar Latino sporting a crew cut entered the diner. He instantly recognized the man as the driver of the gray Chevrolet that had followed Ramon and

Catalina up to East Harlem the other day, the man whom Weiss had later spotted placing a tracer on the couple's not-quite-discreet-enough Hyundai.

His mind quickly grasped the full implications of the man's involvement. If this guy was here to shake down Catalina for the blackmail money, then Montezuma Protection Services, and presumably Carlos Allende, was indeed responsible for placing the hidden camera in the couple's illicit love nest. So why had this man tailed them to El Barrio that day? *I guess Allende wanted to see how Catalina reacted to that first threatening e-mail,* Vaughn surmised. *Maybe he was afraid that she and Ramon would run away for good, instead of submitting to the blackmail?*

In any event, the man went straight to the rear booth and sat down opposite Ramon and Catalina. *"Buenas tardes,"* he greeted them in a thick Mexican accent. "You are here to do business? A wise decision."

Ramon could not contain his anger. *"Hijo de puta!"* He started to rise from his seat, but Catalina restrained him. Vaughn wondered if the bodyguard was surprised that neither Vaughn nor Weiss had shown up to conduct the exchange.

"Please, Ramon," Catalina urged him again. "Please control yourself—for my sake."

The newcomer appeared unfazed by the other man's outburst. "If you do not want to cooperate, I'm sure I can work out an arrangement with the senora's husband."

"No, please!" Catalina exclaimed. "Ramon is just upset, as I'm sure you can understand. This has been a very difficult time for us." She removed her sunglasses and looked at him imploringly. "We definitely want to resolve this matter, believe me!"

The tense exchange was interrupted by the waiter, who arrived to take the man's order. "Nothing for me," the man with the crew cut insisted.

The blackmailer had brought his own laptop, which he opened up across from Catalina's, so that they looked like they were playing a game of Battleship.

Just your typical twenty-first-century payoff, Vaughn reflected. The Internet had certainly made such transactions easier, eliminating the need for suitcases full of unmarked bills. And no more laborious counting to slow things down.

The blackmailer and his victims got down to business. "Do you have the disk?" Catalina asked anxiously.

"You mean this?" the man asked, plucking a

small plastic disk from the breast pocket of his jacket. The tone of his voice suggested that he was taking sadistic pleasure in the woman's discomfort. "As promised, this disk contains the raw, demonstrably undoctored footage of your . . . activities . . . on the date in question." Vaughn couldn't see the man's face from where he was sitting, but he could practically hear the man's salacious leer. "If you desire, we can all watch the show once more."

Vaughn understood the significance of the disk. In these days of computer-generated imagery, when video footage could be digitally manipulated to make Catalina look like she was making love to anyone from Forrest Gump to Roger Rabbit, it was the original, undoctored files that mattered. The ambassador's wife had no guarantee that the blackmailers had not made multiple copies of the sex tape, but she could always insist that any second- or third-generation copies were fakes. Given her compromised position, that was the best that she and Ramon could hope for.

"Cabrón!" Ramon spat. He reached for the disk, but the other man yanked it away from his fingers. Catalina laid her hand upon her lover's arm and gently guided it back to their side of the booth.

"Patience," the blackmailer chided Ramon, replacing the disk in his pocket. "We have business to conduct first." He produced a slip of paper and slid it across the table to Catalina. "Please transfer the agreed-upon sum to this account number."

Swallowing hard, Catalina accepted the note and started typing away at her keyboard. "There," she said finally. "It's done."

"Bueno," the blackmailer said. He consulted his own laptop to confirm that the payment had been made. After a few minutes he shut down the computer and closed its lid, apparently satisfied that all was in order. He got up to leave. "A pleasure doing business with you, senora."

"Aren't you forgetting something?" Ramon growled. He held out his hand. "The disk. Now."

The man made no move to retrieve the disk from his pocket. "I'm afraid there's been a misunderstanding. The amount that Senora Delgado has just provided was merely a down payment." He paused to savor the couple's shocked expressions. "This particular video is worth far more than just 750,000 dollars. My associates and I will be in touch shortly regarding the next payment."

"No!" Catalina gasped. "You can't do this!"

Tears burst from her eyes. "I gave you what you asked for! Every cent!"

The blackmailer could not resist twisting the knife. "You underestimate the truly memorable nature of your passionate performance in the video. I'm sure a woman of your remarkable . . . talents . . . will have no difficulty raising the additional funds." His voice grew ever more taunting. "I know I have enjoyed watching the tape, over and over."

"*Hijo de puta!*" Ramon shouted, loud enough to attract every eye in the restaurant. He reached beneath his jacket and pulled out a gleaming Colt automatic. "Give me one reason why I shouldn't blow your filthy brain to pieces!"

The appearance of the gun sent a shock wave of fear throughout the diner. Waiters and customers gasped in horror before diving beneath their tables or behind the counter.

Except for the guy seated at the counter with Vaughn, who jumped to his feet and pulled out a gun of his own. Before either Vaughn or Ramon realized what was happening, the stranger fired his pistol. A gunshot echoed inside the restaurant and Ramon collapsed against the back of the booth. Blood streamed from his shoulder, and the Colt slipped from his fingers, crashing to the floor.

"Ramon!" Catalina screamed. Her lover's blood was sprayed across her drab overcoat.

The man at the counter took aim at Ramon again, intending to finish him off. Vaughn realized that the man with the crew cut had not been foolish enough to come to the meeting alone. *Damn it*, he thought. *I should have seen this coming!*

"Hey! Look sharp!" he hollered at his neighbor, who turned toward him in surprise. Vaughn grabbed his bowl and hurled the hot soup in the man's face. The blackmailer's accomplice staggered backward, crying out in pain. He fired blindly at Vaughn, missing him by a foot. The stray bullet knocked a blackboard with the diner's daily specials off the wall.

That's enough! Vaughn thought furiously. Moving with a speed that belied his illusory age and infirmity, Vaughn took hold of his cane and swung the wooden stick at the gunman's skull. The stick connected with a resounding *crack* and Vaughn imagined he could almost hear the delicate electronics inside the cane shattering. *Sorry, Marshall.*

The accomplice's baseball cap went flying and he dropped to the floor. *So much for him*, Vaughn thought, kicking the man's gun away from his limp fingers. Drawing his own Beretta, he turned back toward the booth where the deal had gone sour. He saw to his dismay that the blackmailer had taken Catalina hostage, holding the muzzle of a Glock automatic to the woman's temple. Tears streamed down her face, smearing her makeup, while Ramon slumped against the back of the booth, clutching his shoulder.

"Shotgun!" Weiss yelled in Vaughn's ear. "What's happening in there? Do you require assistance?"

"Hold your position, Houdini," Vaughn responded. This situation was volatile enough without throwing another shooter into the mix. "Stand by." He turned his Beretta toward the blackmailer and his hostage. He found it ironic that he, of all people, had to come to the assistance of the ambassador's adulterous wife. "Let the woman go."

The blackmailer shook his head. "I don't know who you are, old man, but you've made a big mistake!" His Glock was pressed against Catalina's skull. "Drop your weapon or the senora is a dead woman."

"Like I care what happens to that cheating whore?" Catalina gasped as though his words were bullets striking into her flesh. "I've dealt with her kind before. Hell, I've killed her kind before. Go ahead and blow her brains out if you like. You'll be doing her husband a favor." He kept the Beretta aimed directly at the other man. "I'm just after the disk," he lied.

The gunman gulped. "You're bluffing," he said uncertainly.

"Try me," Vaughn challenged. Catalina closed her eyes and started praying.

Without warning, Vaughn swung his trigger arm a few inches to the left. A shot rang out and a single bullet blasted the Glock out of the blackmailer's hand, missing Catalina's skull by inches. Gasping in pain, the blackmailer yanked back his empty hand.

"*Caramba!*"

Suddenly finding himself outgunned, the man from Montezuma Protection Services bolted for the front door of the diner. Vaughn tracked him with his gun. "Hold it!" he called out. "Stop or I'll shoot!"

"Help, somebody, please!" Catalina's cries seized Vaughn's attention. Glancing out of the corner of his eye, he saw her holding on to Ramon's hand with a panicked expression on her face. The injured bodyguard's own face was ashen. Blood continued to stream from the bullet wound in his shoulder. "He's dying! Help him, please!"

Vaughn realized he could either see to Ramon or chase after the blackmailer; he couldn't do both. *Damn!* he thought, lowering his gun. He couldn't let the bodyguard die, no matter what he had done with another man's wife. "Shotgun to Houdini. You've got company. Take him down."

"I'm on it, buddy!" Weiss replied.

Trusting that his partner could handle the blackmailer on his own, Vaughn holstered his Beretta and dashed over to the booth. *"Gracias!"* Catalina sobbed, moving out of Vaughn's way as he inspected Ramon's injury.

Judging from the color and flow of the blood, he guessed that the bodyguard had been lucky and no arteries had been severed. Had this been an arterial wound, the blood would have been much brighter and jetting from the bullet hole. There was no exit wound, so the bullet was still wedged inside the man's shoulder. Blood loss struck Vaughn as the most serious threat, followed closely by shock, so he unwound the scarf around his neck and used it as a field dressing, applying pressure to the wound to halt the bleeding. "Call 911!" he shouted to the nearest waiter, who was just starting to emerge from beneath a table. "And get me a first-aid kit!"

Ramon's eyes widened as he recognized Vaughn's voice. "You?" he said in confusion, baffled by the agent's false face. "The man in the car?" His voice was weak and halting. "But . . . I don't understand . . ."

"Yeah, it's me," Vaughn confirmed tersely. "See, I told you I wasn't the one responsible for that video."

This was too much for Ramon. His eyelids drooped and he sagged against the padded back of the booth, too overcome with this realization to probe further. His shallow breathing and clammy skin suggested that he was going into shock.

"Is he going to be okay?" Catalina asked, hovering behind Vaughn.

"Probably." Vaughn had seen a lot of gunshot wounds in his time, including a few in his own flesh, and Ramon's injury didn't strike him as life-threatening, provided that the bodyguard received medical attention soon. "Trust me, I've seen worse."

Like the time Irina Derevko shot Weiss . . .

The door swung open and his partner marched

the blackmailer back into the diner at gunpoint. The fetid pink comforter had been left outside, but Vaughn could still smell Weiss's homeless disguise all the way across the restaurant. Weiss's charge trudged glumly in front of him, his hands clasped behind his head. Weiss's scarf had come loose, exposing his jubilant grin.

"Anybody order a blackmailer?"

Vaughn glanced over at the blackmailer's partner, who was starting to stir on the floor in front of the counter. "Come closer," he beckoned to Catalina. He shifted to the right to allow her to slide into the booth beside him. He placed her hand on the wadded-up scarf against her lover's punctured shoulder. "Keep pressing down on that," he instructed her, "until the ambulance gets here."

"Sí, claro. Gracias," she said, taking his place. "It's all right, Ramon," she cooed to the injured bodyguard. "I'm here for you, baby. I'm not going anywhere."

Vaughn slid out of the booth and walked over to where the accomplice was still sprawled on the floor, a nasty bump on his head. He confiscated the man's gun and pulled a set of handcuffs out of the pocket of his baggy Army surplus coat. "Stay down there," he warned the stunned gunman as he cuffed him to his stool.

Weiss nodded approvingly. "Not bad for a senior citizen." He handcuffed his own prisoner to a coat stand. "How's retirement treating you?"

"Very funny," Vaughn replied. "Look who's talking, Stinky."

Satisfied the downed bad guy was taken care of, Vaughn walked over to the blackmailer, who was glowering at him silently. "I believe you have something that doesn't belong to you."

Vaughn extracted the disk from the man's breast pocket.

"What are you going to do with that?" Weiss asked.

Vaughn wasn't sure. He held in his hand conclusive evidence of Catalina Delgado's adultery, but what business was that of his? Sloane would probably want him to hold on to the disk, to use as leverage against the ambassador's wife at some point in the future, yet Vaughn just felt like wiping his hands of the entire sordid affair. True, Catalina had betrayed her husband, but he was starting to doubt whether she had anything to do with Niccolo Genovese. Considering what Sydney had learned from Rivera about

Delgado's underworld connections, it sounded like there were bigger issues in play than a cheating wife.

And, she's not Lauren.

Grimly, he walked back to the booth and handed the disk to Catalina. "Here," he said without emotion. "You bought and paid for this."

"Gracias, senor! For everything!" Accepting the disk with her free hand, she stared up at Vaughn with teary eyes. Her voice caught in her throat. "What you said before, when that man threatened to kill me, you . . . you were very convincing."

Vaughn recalled the cruel words he had flung in her direction. "If I were you, Senora Delgado, I would have a talk with your husband."

He heard sirens approaching.

"Let's get out of here," he said to Weiss, inclined to let the NYPD deal with their captured prisoners. He handed the accomplice's gun over to the dumbfounded waiter behind the counter. "Keep an eye on these jerks," he told the rattled civilian. "They shouldn't give you any more trouble. And thanks for the crackers."

CHAPTER 14

VENICE, ITALY

Famously described by Napoleon as the "drawing room of Europe," the Piazza San Marco was a spacious square at the heart of Venice's winding canals, dominated by the Byzantine splendor of St. Mark's Basilica. The vast church, with its ornate domes and glittering blue-and-gold mosaics, overlooked the long rectangular piazza, which was bordered by elegant cafés and galleries. The Doge's Palace, a colonnaded Gothic masterpiece that once housed the city's secular powers, rose up beside the basilica, placing church and state within arm's reach of each other.

The square was already full of masked men and women decked out in elaborate, brightly colored costumes with sequins, silk, lace, velvet, and feathers taking part in the yearly celebration of Carnival. Papier-mâché masks, inspired by the traditions and characters of the commedia dell'arte, hid the faces of various Harlequins, Pantaloons, and Columbines who pranced about the square. An elevated stage had been erected at the western end of the piazza, where a string quartet played Vivaldi for the sightseers seated at the open-air cafés lining the square. Vendors sold small sacks of birdseed to tourists, who were swarmed with voracious pigeons the minute they cracked open the bags.

The garish spectacle was not to Jack Bristow's taste, but he had to admit that Carnival provided both anonymity and the relative security of a crowd. No wonder The Smoke had chosen this time and place for their appointment once Kao Yun persuaded Niccolo Genovese's mysterious partner to meet with Jack, who hoped to finally discover the late assassin's connection to the Mexican Consulate in New York.

Sydney is operating in the dark over there, he thought uneasily. *She needs reliable intel.*

Jack sat at an outdoor table in front of Quadri Café, waiting for The Smoke to arrive. He wore a conservative gray suit and his face was covered by a bone-white mask with a long pointed beak. The traditional Venetian design represented the plague-doctor of medieval Europe, who had worn a similar face protector as a precaution against the Black Death. A pair of round spectacles were painted on the mask; typically the plague doctor's glasses were black, but on Jack's mask the spectacles were a vivid shade of red. The variation was deliberate so that The Smoke would be able to pick Jack out of the crowd.

Jack's eyes probed the square. Although his own mask had been prearranged, as one of the terms of the meeting he had no idea what sort of disguise The Smoke had adopted for the occasion. Through Kao Yun, the elusive figure had insisted that he (or she) make the initial contact at the designated site. Surrounded by so many cloaked strangers, any one of whom might be the associate of an infamous assassin, Jack could not help feeling somewhat exposed.

Thankfully, he was not alone. "Raptor to Evergreen," he murmured behind his mask. "Are you in position?"

"That's an affirmative, Raptor," Nadia answered. "I have you in view."

Jack peered across the teeming square at the campanile, the historic bell tower standing near the southeast corner of the piazza, across from the Doge's Palace. Rising more than three hundred feet above the square, the celebrated belfry was topped by a golden weathervane. Jack could not make out Nadia among the throng milling about the base of the tower, but he knew she was there, decked out as a female Harlequin in a form-fitting costume adorned with a pattern of black, white, and scarlet diamonds. Magnifying lenses in her own mask would allow her to observe the meeting from a distance.

The bells of the campanile tolled three, and Jack began to fear that The Smoke would be a no-show. He hoped it would not be necessary to exert more pressure on Kao Yun to ensure a meeting. Time was too short to waste precious hours bullying the recalcitrant Chinese spymaster, especially with Sydney at risk in Manhattan.

He was on the verge of giving up when a masked stranger approached his table. A white half mask covered the upper part of the unidentifiable man's face, with a black veil cloaking his mouth and jaw. A black tricorn hat was perched atop his head, completing a traditional disguise known as a *bauta.* The stranger's black velvet gloves clutched a striped candy-colored wand, as well as a sealed bag of birdseed. The flamboyant costume made it difficult to determine his age or ethnicity.

"They say Venice is sinking," he informed Jack.

"Then we had best learn to swim," Jack replied, completing the predetermined exchange.

The masked figure nodded in satisfaction, yet did not sit down. "Please stand up," he instructed Jack, brandishing his wand. His voice betrayed an Italian accent. "I need to make sure that you haven't violated our agreement."

Jack rose from his chair and allowed The Smoke (as he assumed the stranger to be) to sweep his wand along the contours of the agent's body, scanning him for concealed weapons or wires. As promised, Jack had come to the piazza unarmed, and he was confident that APO's miniaturized comms would evade all but the most invasive of searches.

"Satisfied?" he asked.

The Smoke lowered his wand. "I suppose." He remained standing, as though hesitant to commit himself to the meeting. His eyes darted from side to side, anticipating an ambush. Jack was glad that Nadia was nowhere nearby.

"Why don't you sit down?" Jack suggested.

With visible reluctance, The Smoke took a seat across from Jack, placing his wand on the table. "Forgive my nerves," he apologized. "I am unaccustomed to such encounters. My late partner was the public face of our joint business."

"My condolences on your loss," Jack said. He neglected to mention that his own daughter was indirectly responsible for Genovese's demise. "Thank you for agreeing to meet with me."

"Prego." The masked man struck Jack as distinctly twitchy. He kept glancing about in a jittery manner, while his fingers toyed restlessly with the bag of birdseed. "What is this all about, signore? I must inform you, I considered myself semiretired these days, now that Niccolo is gone. I am only taking on a few very special commissions, which require little active participation on my part. It was Niccolo who actually carried out our assignments in the field. I preferred to remain behind the

scenes, handling the logistics and equipment."

"You were the brains of the operation," Jack translated. "As it happens, I am not at all interested in engaging your services. All I'm after is information regarding one of your previous commissions, the one concerning the Mexican Consulate in New York City."

The other man shifted uncomfortably in his chair. "I'm afraid I have no idea what you're talking about."

"Don't play games with me," Jack warned him. "We know that Genovese was in touch with someone at the consulate. What I want to know is who."

"Please, signore!" The Smoke protested. "You must understand that the names of my clients are strictly confidential. Discretion is everything in this business."

"So is self-preservation." Jack allowed a menacing tone to creep into his voice. "You would be well advised to cooperate, unless you want to end up like your late colleague."

The Smoke stiffened. "Are you threatening me? You forget we are in a public place."

"Wearing masks," Jack reminded him. His merciless eyes peered from behind the mask of the plague doctor. "All I need is a minute to kill you with my bare hands. Then I can simply discard this ridiculous mask and disappear into the crowd before anyone around us even realizes that you are dead." The Smoke started to rise from his seat, but Jack laid a restraining hand upon his arm. "Don't even think about trying to get away."

"Let go of me!" the other man yelped. He thrust the bag of birdseed beneath his veil and ripped open the small paper sack with his teeth, then tossed the contents of the bag onto Jack, who was immediately besieged by dozens of frantic pigeons. The birds' countless wings roared in Jack's ears as he was inundated by warm, feathery bodies. The hungry birds pecked insistently at his mask and clothes, searching for the seeds lodged in the folds of his jacket and slacks. Jack flailed wildly with his free arm, trying to bat the pigeons away, but thanks to the thousands of tourists who fed them daily, the birds had long since lost their fear of man. For every pigeon Jack knocked aside, three more swooped in to take its place. He could barely see through the swarm of birds engulfing him.

"Get away! Shoo!" he shouted at them.

Taking advantage of the distraction, The Smoke

yanked his arm free and jumped to his feet. He turned and ran from the table, heading east toward the basilica. *Damn it!* Jack thought, furious at himself for not anticipating the pigeon attack. He rose abruptly to his feet, overturning the small table as he did so, and hastily brushed the remaining seeds from his chest before taking off in pursuit of the fleeing criminal. Greedy pigeons chased after him, their wings beating excitedly. "The target is on the run!" he alerted Nadia as he sprinted across the square, bulldozing his way through the crowd. The beaked mask restricted his vision and he angrily tossed it aside. "Prepare to intercept!"

"I see him, Raptor!" Nadia confirmed. "Do you know where he's going?"

Jack was grateful for the backup, even if Nadia was Irina's illegitimate daughter. Up ahead, The Smoke raced into the Piazzetta dei Leoni, a small square on the northern side of the basilica. Jack recalled that the Rio di Palazzo, one of the city's many interconnecting canals, was only a few blocks farther east. No doubt The Smoke was fully aware of that.

"He may be heading for the canal!" Jack warned Nadia, breathing hard. Although in excellent shape for a man his age, he was getting too old to chase suspects on foot like this, especially when he suspected they were younger than he was. Still, he continued to sprint through the crowd, determined not to let their only lead slip away. "I'll keep on his tail. See if you can head him off before he reaches the lagoon!"

"Understood," Nadia responded. Her voice held a questioning note. "Are you sure you don't want me to take over the chase?"

"Just go!" he barked irritably.

He pursued The Smoke through the tiny piazzetta into the Calle Canonica, a narrow street running alongside the Patriarchal Palace at the rear of the basilica. Startled revelers and sightseers dove out of the way of the masked fugitive and his pursuer to let the two men dash by. Jack was glad to let The Smoke clear the path for him, since it gave him a much-needed edge on the other man. Laughter, jeers, and profanities, in multiple languages, followed the men as they forced their way through the crush of Carnival celebrants.

After all this, he thought testily, *I'm going to enjoy persuading him to talk.*

Soon he glimpsed the murky green waters of

the Rio di Palazzo up ahead. A gondolier, wearing the traditional straw hat, striped shirt, and black trousers, stood by an upright mooring post, fending off a young American couple who couldn't understand why he wouldn't let them hire him for a ride. His glossy black gondola floated upon the canal behind him, its dark lacquered finish gleaming in the sunlight. "C'mon," the American youth argued. "It's our honeymoon. Give us a break." He held out a handful of euros, a confused expression on his face. "I thought this is what you guys do."

The gondolier's eyes lighted up as he spotted The Smoke racing toward him. Obviously, The Smoke had arranged to have a boat waiting for him in case he needed to make a swift escape. The gondolier hastily untied the rope around the striped post. *"Fretta!"*

The Smoke jumped into the bobbing gondola. "Hey!" the newlywed husband protested as the masked man dropped onto one of the upholstered stools in the middle of the boat. "We were here first!"

The impatient oarsman shoved the American man into the canal, where he landed with a splash. Cold water sprayed his young wife, who shrieked in dismay. The gondolier ignored her as he climbed into the boat after his employer. Jack pressed on, with a final burst of speed, hoping to catch up with the gondola before it got away. He wasn't looking forward to taking on both men at once, but The Smoke didn't strike him as much of a fighter. *I can still do this!* he thought stubbornly. *I have to. For Sydney and the mission.*

But instead of taking up his oar, the gondolier crouched at the rear of the boat and threw back a dark blanket, exposing an electronic control panel. He flipped a few switches and the roar of a concealed engine provoked startled looks from people strolling alongside the canal. *No!* Jack thought, slowing to a halt at the very edge of the canal. He clenched his fists in frustration as the motorized gondola pulled away from its moorings and zoomed through the canal. As he'd expected, the speeding craft headed south toward the lagoon surrounding the main island. Once the boat reached the open water, there would be no way to catch it. The Smoke and his accomplice could escape to any of the smaller islands or even to the mainland.

"I lost him, Evergreen," he reported bitterly. "He's heading your way."

It was all up to Nadia now.

* * *

Per Jack's instructions, Nadia abandoned her post beneath the campanile and ran south, hoping to head The Smoke off at the end of the canal, where the Rio di Palazzo gave way to larger canals leading out into the lagoon. She agreed with Jack's assessment of the situation; if their target took to the water, he would doubtless aim for the lagoon rather than risk getting bogged down in the city's maze of narrow canals.

That's what I would do, she thought.

She turned off the magnifying lenses in her burgundy leather domino mask. She was glad that she wasn't wearing an elaborate gown or flowing robe like many of the other costumed revelers. Her diamond-patterned bodysuit permitted her plenty of freedom of movement. An Italian leather handbag was slung over her shoulder.

The Doge's Palace was on her left as she raced across the Piazzetta San Marco, a smaller square adjacent to the larger piazza. Ahead, beyond two tall granite columns, the tail end of the Grand Canal stretched out before her, many times larger than the Rio di Palazzo. A small armada of gondolas, many covered by protective blue tarps, were moored along the canal. In the distance, on the other side of the Grand Canal, the island of San Giorgio was home to a venerable church and Benedictine monastery, complete with a scenic bell tower of its own. The Grand Canal flowed past the island before merging with the even larger Canal di San Marco and the open water beyond.

Nadia had no time to enjoy the view. Reaching the end of the piazzetta, she turned left toward the canal and dashed past the southern facade of the palace. The Ponte della Paglia, a stone footbridge spanning the Rio di Palazzo, was straight ahead of her, and as she sprinted for the bridge she prayed that she wouldn't see a boat shoot out of the canal before she got to it.

We've come too far to let The Smoke slip through our fingers now!

Reaching the bridge, she took the steps two at a time until she reached the midpoint of the white stone arch, which was high enough above the water to allow a gondolier a decent amount of head room. She turned north to face the canal, her back to the vast expanse of water behind her. Several yards in front of her, Venice's infamous Bridge of Sighs blocked her view of the Rio di Palazzo. The enclosed, windowless bridge led from the Doge's Palace to the ancient prison cells across the canal; its name evoked the fearful lamentations of those condemned to torture and execution. Nadia, who had seen more than her fair share of torture chambers, could not help sympathizing with the poor souls who had once trodden across the bridge.

Drawing a loaded Beretta from her handbag, she climbed up onto the rail of the stone archway. She heard the roar of a motorboat drawing nearer.

She didn't have to wait long. A sleek black gondola, spraying a tail of frothy water behind it, came zipping beneath the Bridge of Sighs. Nadia spotted The Smoke seated in the boat and took aim with her Beretta before remembering that they needed the target alive to answer questions. *"Fermate!"* she yelled at the gondola, straining to be heard over the roar of the engine. She fired a warning shot into the water in front of the boat. "Stop!"

But the gondola didn't even slow down, giving Nadia only seconds to react. As the speeding craft threatened to disappear beneath the bridge upon which she stood, Nadia leaped, gun in hand, from the rail.

She landed feet first in the gondola, almost

capsizing it. The startled gondolier pulled a small knife from his breast pocket and flung it at Nadia's head. She deftly ducked the blade and fired her Beretta once. Blood erupted from the man's chest and he toppled backward into the canal, dead before he hit the water. Cold green waves took on a reddish hue as the gondolier sank beneath the surface of the canal.

Nadia barely spared a moment to regret the killing. *A necessary casualty,* she assured herself. The gondolier had attacked her first and was in the employ of a known assassin. *He had it coming.*

Unmanned, the engine-powered gondola veered off course, scraping against the starboard wall of the canal. The jolt almost knocked Nadia off her feet, but she managed to maintain her balance. She turned her Beretta toward The Smoke as she dropped onto her knees and took control of the rudder. "Don't move!" she warned the masked man, who flinched at the sight of her smoking gun. "And keep your hands where I can see them."

Jack's voice spoke in her ear. "Evergreen, report! I heard a gunshot."

"That was me," she informed him under her breath. "Venice is minus a gondolier." Her eyes remained locked on The Smoke. "Meanwhile, I've acquired the target. Meet me at the rendezvous point, after I've had a few minutes with our friend here."

"Will do," he agreed. "Good work."

Nadia was glad to have impressed Sydney's father. Keeping her gun trained on The Smoke, she steered the gondola beneath the Ponte della Paglia and out into the Grand Canal, then headed out away from the main island in search of a little privacy. Once she judged they had gone far enough, about halfway to the island of San Giorgio, she killed the engine and let the boat drift on the current.

"Now then," she addressed her unwilling passenger, "I believe my partner had just asked you a question. Who was Genovese in touch with at the Mexican Consulate?"

The Smoke glanced over the side of the gondola, as if considering taking his chances in the frigid waters. For all he knew, hypothermia might be preferable to what his captor had in mind.

"I wouldn't think about it if I were you," she cautioned him. Abandoning the rudder, she moved along the middle of the boat until she was only inches away from The Smoke. "It's a long swim back, especially with several ounces of lead weighing you down."

"Please!" he begged her. His voice grew increasingly hysterical as he spoke. "You don't understand. If anyone finds out I divulged the name of a client, my life won't be worth a cent!"

Nadia didn't have time to argue with him. She smacked her Beretta hard across the masked man's face. Papier-mâché cracked beneath the blow. "That's not my problem," she informed him coldly. Nadia considered herself a good person, but she couldn't deny she had a dark side that proved to be useful sometimes. Her slender fingers reached beneath his lacy veil and ripped the crumpled mask from his face. "Let's get a look at you."

To her surprise, Niccolo Genovese stared back at her.

What the hell? she thought, rendered momentarily speechless. APO had confirmed Genovese's death in London, and Sydney herself had seen the assassin cut his own throat right before her eyes. So how was he now alive and well, attending Carnival in Venice?

An explanation occurred to her, and she tugged at his collar, exposing his throat. There was no trace of a scar.

"A twin?" she guessed. "Niccolo's brother?"

The Smoke nodded fearfully, his Adam's apple bobbing like a yo-yo. His face was already turning purple where Nadia had pistol-whipped him. "Salvatore," he volunteered. "Salvatore Genovese."

Of course, she thought. *No wonder Niccolo committed suicide rather than let himself be captured and interrogated. He was protecting his twin brother.*

"Interesting," she observed. "But that still doesn't answer my question." She drew back her gun arm, ready to strike him again if necessary. "Talk . . . while you still have some teeth."

Again, Salvatore hesitated, which made her wonder just what he was so determined to hide. "This is insane!" he bleated. Despite the cool temperature, he was sweating like a man in a sauna. "Who the hell are you, anyway?"

"My name doesn't matter," she told him. She smacked his face again with the Beretta and he yelped in pain. This time there was no papier-mâché to soften the blow. Cold steel collided with fragile flesh and bone. "All you need to know is that I am the only daughter of Arvin Sloane and Irina Derevko." She stared into his eyes without a hint of mercy or compassion. "I'm told I inherited my kindly nature from both of them."

Her parents' names put the fear of God into him, just as she'd hoped they would. Salvatore's eyes widened in terror and his battered face went pale beneath its swelling bruises. Blood gushed from his nose and lips. "All right!" he gasped. "No more, *per favore*! I'll tell you whatever you want to know!"

That's more like it, she thought. "Give me the name."

"I never knew the name!" he insisted. "The client was anonymous. I'm telling you the truth!"

Nadia believed him. He was too frightened to lie to her. "What was the deal, then? What did the client want from you?"

Salvatore swallowed hard before answering. "A neutron bomb. Small enough to fit into a briefcase or diplomatic pouch." He flinched in anticipation of her reaction. "Powerful enough to kill everyone in a large building."

Nadia couldn't believe her ears. A neutron bomb? She now understood why Salvatore, aka The Smoke, had been so reluctant to talk about this particular commission. Nuclear terrorism, even on a limited scale, was not something the authorities took lightly.

"Why did the client want this bomb?" she demanded. "What's the plan?"

Salvatore threw up his hands. "I have no idea. Our job was just to construct the weapon and deliver it on time." A note of pride entered his voice. "Quite a technical challenge, really. Not everyone could have done it. . . ."

His use of the past tense sent a chill down her spine. "Don't tell me you've already delivered the bomb!"

"A week ago," he confirmed, wincing in anticipation of another blow. "Well ahead of the client's deadline."

This was sounding worse and worse. "Which was?"

"Twenty-four hours ago."

Oh my God! Nadia thought. She leaned back against the side of the gondola, aghast. If Salvatore's nameless client needed the bomb by yesterday, then an attack of some sort could take place at any time, anywhere. Perhaps at the United Nations or the consulate.

In a moment of horror, Nadia realized that her sister could be at ground zero this very second.

Sydney!

CHAPTER 15

MEXICAN CONSULATE

Sydney stormed into Rivera's office and closed the door. "We need to talk . . . now."

She quickly briefed the deputy on what Nadia had just learned in Venice. The CIA had verified Rivera's story regarding CISEN, so she assumed she could trust him. *At the moment,* she thought, *I need all the help I can get.*

"A neutron bomb?" he responded, a stunned expression on his face. "Are you sure this intel is reliable?"

"I'm sure." She didn't mention that the

information came straight from her own father and half sister. "My colleagues turned Salvatore Genovese over to Interpol for further questioning, but they're convinced he was telling the truth. It's hard to imagine that he would lie about something like this. What could be worse than confessing to manufacturing a miniature atomic bomb—and providing it to an unknown terrorist?"

Rivera winced at the thought. "I see what you mean," he conceded. "And your people have no idea what the bomb is intended for?"

"No," Sydney admitted. "Only that the buyer needed the bomb by yesterday, which means we're looking at an immediate threat." She recalled with relief that Mercedes was nowhere near the UN or the consulate this morning; the girl was researching a homework assignment at the library with her bodyguard close at hand. "We could be sitting on top of the bomb at this very minute."

To his credit, the Mexican agent did not immediately flee the building. Instead he sank back into his padded executive chair. "So what's our next move?"

Sydney had already figured that out. "We need to get into that safe in the ambassador's office

ASAP. If Delgado has any connection to the bomb, there might be a clue in there. At this point, we have to start eliminating suspects as fast as humanly possible." She paced restlessly in front of his desk. "Where is Delgado now?"

"In the video-conferencing room downstairs," Rivera said. "Observing some sort of award ceremony being held over at the UN." The deputy glanced down at an itinerary on his desk. "He asked not to be disturbed."

Sydney realized that Rivera had to be talking about the event honoring Sloane; Dixon had mentioned that that sham of a ceremony was being held this morning. *How ironic is that?*

"Perfect," she said. "Just get me into that office. I can do the rest."

Rivera nodded in agreement. "I think I can manage that."

A few minutes later she and Rivera stepped out into the hall. Was it just her imagination, or did their emergence from behind closed doors provoke snickers and knowing glances from the consulate's staff? Sydney suspected that either Allende or the members of his security team had been spreading rumors about that embarrassing incident in her room the other night.

Big deal, she thought. So what if everyone in the consulate thought she was a slut? She had bigger things to worry about right now than the reputation of her alias. Specifically, an unaccounted-for neutron bomb. *I can't let this city endure another terrorist attack. It's already suffered so much. . . .*

Sydney and Rivera came to a halt in front of Victor Delgado's office. "Thank you for coming to me with this, Ms. Talbot," Rivera declared loudly enough to be easily overheard. "The ambassador will want to speak with you at his first opportunity. Please wait here until he can see you. I'll see to it that you are not disturbed."

"Thank you so much, Senor Rivera," she said soberly, a grave expression on her face. If any onlookers assumed that she had serious matters to discuss with Ambassador Delgado, perhaps concerning Mercedes's grades or the attempted kidnapping, Sydney was not about to deprive them of such notions. "I knew that the ambassador would want to hear about this as soon as possible."

Rivera led her into the private office and closed the door behind them. "I think that went well." He walked over to the bookshelf where the safe was hidden and marked the spot by pulling a bound volume out of alignment with the other books around it. "Do you want me to watch the door?"

Sydney shook her head. "I'd rather you went downstairs and kept an eye on Delgado. Make sure that he doesn't get bored with the ceremony and head back here. Delay him if you have to. Give me ten to fifteen minutes at least." He started to go, but another thought occurred to her. "Wait a second. What about Allende?" The last thing she wanted was to have the paranoid security chief walk in on her while she was cracking the safe. *Even if he is a crook and a blackmailer.*

"Don't worry," Rivera assured her. "He had a nine o'clock meeting with the chief of police to discuss the incident in the subway. We're not expecting him back until later this morning."

Good to know, Sydney thought.

She waited until Rivera left, then dropped her handbag on top of Delgado's desk, not far from the phone someone had used to contact Niccolo Genovese. Opening the bag, she removed a compact device disguised as an ordinary electronic notebook. Weiss, unwilling to risk even a brush with Allende's henchmen since showing his face in East Harlem, had taped the device beneath the sink in the restroom of a nearby coffee shop, where Sydney had retrieved it while on a lunch break. Its innocuous appearance had easily fooled the consulate's security guards.

I knew I was going to need this, she thought. She had requested the device after her first, aborted attempt to search the ambassador's office, but, given the increased security at the consulate, she had lacked the opportunity to use it until now. Learning about the bomb, however, had forced her hand. *I can't afford to wait any longer.*

Moving quickly, she peeled away the PDA's false exterior to expose a rectangular black box about the size of a Hershey bar, featuring an eight-figure digital display. She rushed over to the bookshelf, where she cleared away a couple of volumes of literary camouflage to expose the wall safe behind the books. It was a new Model W310 Midas, from the looks of it. Sydney all but whistled in appreciation. Victor Delgado had spared no expense when it came to protecting his secrets; the W310 was state of the art, with the locking mechanism protected by a dense carburized hardplate, and a spring-loaded relock as a backup. An electronic keypad offered thousands of possible combinations. The safe's unblemished matte black finish suggested that it had been freshly installed to replace the one Rivera had so ineptly tampered with.

Sydney recalled the blaring siren she had heard outside the window a week ago. *Let's not have a replay of that debacle,* she resolved. Not that she was worried about triggering the alarm by accident. *CISEN's good, but they don't have Marshall. . . .*

She attached the device to the front of the safe and turned it on. She braced herself for the siren, just in case, but all she heard was a steady electronic hum as the computerized safecracking mechanism used a wireless connection to run through every possible combination at breathtaking speed. The numbers on the gadget's digital display flashed by in a blur. "Phoenix here," she updated headquarters. "I'm attempting to open the package now."

"I read you, Phoenix," Marshall replied. "Boy, is it lonely around here today. Sloane's in the Big Apple with you guys. Jack and Nadia are still flying back from Italy. I feel like I've got the whole place to myself, especially this early in the morning." Sydney realized that it was barely 8 A.M. in Los

Angeles. "Any chance you folks are coming home soon?"

"Here's hoping," Sydney said. *Assuming I don't get zapped by a neutron bomb first.* "One way or another, this mission may be over before we know it."

With nothing to do but wait for Marshall's pride and joy to do its work, she leaned back against the edge of the ambassador's desk. *What if I don't find anything incriminating?* she worried. *Then what am I supposed to do?* The bomb could be anywhere, and the CIA could hardly evacuate both the UN and the consulate indefinitely, especially when they didn't even know the intended time or place of the bombing. *For all we know, the attack is supposed to occur somewhere else entirely.*

An electronic beep signaled that the correct combination had been located. "Thank you, Merlin," she whispered. "I think we have a winner."

She tugged on the handle of the safe, and the thick metal door swung open without so much as a creak. She peered into the safe and her eyes widened in surprise.

Along with several folders of papers, a silver-plated trophy occupied the safe. A sculpted globe rested atop a polished obsidian base bearing an inscribed silver plaque. The shadowy interior of the vault made it hard to read the engraving.

Huh? Sydney thought. Why would Delgado keep this trophy locked away in his state-of-the-art safe, instead of displaying it on his bookshelves with the rest of his distinguished awards and citations? She lifted the trophy out of the safe and read the inscription:

To Arvin Sloane
Presented on behalf of the United Nations
World Food Programme
in recognition of his outstanding
accomplishments in feeding the hungry of
the world

Sloane's award? Sydney didn't understand. Wasn't Sloane supposed to be receiving his so-called tribute over at the UN complex right now? According to Rivera, Ambassador Delgado was currently downstairs watching the ceremony via closed-circuit TV. So what was Sloane's trophy doing here?

"Anything interesting in the safe?" Marshall asked. "Relevant to the mission, I mean."

"I'm not sure," she answered. "Hold on."

Puzzled, she put the trophy down on the desk. She removed a dossier from the safe and began flipping through it quickly. It took her a second to realize what she was looking at, and then a sense of horror came over her.

"Oh my God," she whispered.

The dossier contained a top-secret report on an incident Sydney recalled only too well. Almost four years ago a suitcase-size neutron bomb had killed more than sixty innocent people in a church in Mexico City. The experimental device had raised the victims' body temperatures by two thousand degrees in a matter of seconds, reducing them to ashes while leaving the church intact. Sydney had personally witnessed the immediate aftermath of the massacre; the ghastly image of those carbonized bodies was seared forever into her memory.

She also remembered who had ordered the attack, back before he had reinvented himself as a humanitarian and secret CIA asset.

Arvin Sloane.

"The trophy!" she said. It all made sense now, in a twisted sort of way. Although Sloane's involvement in the church bombing had never been made public, Delgado must have used his government and underworld connections to learn who was responsible for the Mexico City attack. *Now he's planning to kill Sloane in retaliation,* she guessed, *with the use of another neutron bomb intended as poetic justice.*

Her gaze was drawn to the painting of the Mexican cathedral mounted on the other side of the office—a daily reminder of the horror Sloane had inflicted on Delgado's nation four years ago. Sydney shuddered again at the memory. The folder in her hand held many grisly photos of the cremated remains of the victims: more than sixty innocent men, women, and children, burned alive from the inside out.

Who could blame Delgado for wanting to avenge their deaths? For one endless moment she considered telling Marshall that she was mistaken, that she hadn't found anything conclusive in the safe, but then her sense of duty asserted itself. There were more lives than Sloane's at stake. Who knew what the range of the bomb was? She understood Delgado's thirst for revenge, but at this moment everyone at the United Nations, including Dixon, was in mortal danger.

Sydney closed the file and contemplated the trophy on the desk. If the real award was here, then the trophy at the ceremony surely contained the miniature neutron bomb constructed by Salvatore Genovese at Delgado's request. The ambassador must have switched the trophies when no one was looking. And now he was downstairs in the video-conferencing room, ready to watch Sloane die.

"Phoenix?" Marshall asked her over the comm-link. "What was that about a trophy?"

Just my luck, she thought bitterly. *I have to save the life of the man I hate most in the world.*

"The bomb is in the trophy," she alerted Marshall. "At the UN." According to Rivera, the ceremony was already underway. Sloane could be receiving his award at any minute. "Patch me through to Outrigger right now!"

Dixon couldn't believe what he was seeing, but he couldn't look away.

As the General Assembly was not presently in session, the award ceremony was being held in the vast domed hall where the Assembly usually met. Rows of leather-covered desks faced the raised speaker's platform at the front of the huge auditorium, which encompassed a full three floors of the building, including the balcony. The emblem of the United Nations, a circular map of the world flanked by olive branches, was emblazoned on the sloping wall behind the speaker's rostrum and podium. The seventy-five-foot ceiling gave the room the feel of a vast cathedral. Abstract murals adorned each side of the General Assembly Hall.

At full capacity, the hall could accommodate more than twenty-one hundred people, including the delegates and their advisors, agency heads, members of the media, special guests, and other observers. This morning's event was not quite so well attended; Dixon estimated that the hall was about one-third full, which meant that seven hundred people had shown up to honor Arvin Sloane for his selfless contributions to humanity.

Dixon was glad he had a strong stomach.

The undercover agent sat in a glass-enclosed booth overlooking the hall. Although Ambassador Delgado was not physically present at the ceremony below, Dixon had been enlisted to provide a simultaneous Spanish translation for the various Latin American relief organizations attending the event. A pitcher of water rested on the counter in front of him, along with a glass, a microphone, and, where possible, advance copies of the text of the various speeches to be delivered. Earphones allowed him to listen carefully to each speaker's remarks, just in case they deviated from the prepared texts.

The ceremony had started less than an hour ago, and already Dixon had been forced to endure the grotesque spectacle of one speaker after another parading to the podium to praise Sloane as one of the world's great humanitarians. That Dixon then had to repeat those egregious remarks in Spanish only added to his growing discomfort. The faces of Sloane's victims—Diane, Danny Hecht, Francie Calfo, among others—passed through his mind, providing a damning rebuttal to the flattering words emanating from the podium.

This is the very definition of obscenity, he brooded darkly. It was almost enough to make him doubt that there was any justice in the world at all. He constantly had to remind himself that there were larger issues at stake. *We're here to prevent an assassination, and God knows what else.*

Dozens of feet below, a representative of the World Food Programme finished introducing today's guest of honor. Dixon stared balefully as Sloane walked out onto the stage, receiving an enthusiastic round of applause. As usual, the insidious spymaster was impeccably dressed. Wearing a tailored black suit, he stepped toward the podium to receive his award.

Dixon was tempted to avert his eyes. *I'm not sure I can watch this.*

"Outrigger!" Sydney's voice spoke loudly in his ear, drowning out the muffled applause coming through his earphones. "We have an emergency!"

The urgency in her tone seized his attention, and he listened with mounting alarm as she hurriedly explained her theory regarding the bomb in the trophy. *Good Lord!* he thought. His eyes zeroed in on the silver trophy in the speaker's hands. If Sydney was right, the bomb could detonate at any second. His heart skipped a beat as he grasped that his own life was in immediate danger, but then he forced himself to concentrate on the big picture. Everyone in the building could be dead within seconds. He remembered the lines of tourists, the kids on field trips who showed up at the Visitors Entrance every morning . . . *Dear God . . . no . . . !*

"I'm on it!" he declared. He hit the fire-alarm

button on the panel in front of him, and an ear-splitting siren sounded throughout the entire building. His fingers danced over the controls next to his microphone, patching him into the hall's public address system. "Please evacuate the building immediately," he urged the audience below. "This is not a drill!"

Onstage, about to accept his award, Sloane looked up in surprise. Not taking any chances, he immediately spun around and marched briskly toward the nearest exit, leaving the deadly trophy behind. Dixon experienced mixed feelings as he saw his wife's murderer disappear into the mob of confused and frightened people swarming the exits. *You owe me, Sloane,* he thought gravely. *And someday I'm going to collect.*

In the meantime, there was still a neutron bomb to deal with. Dixon realized there was no time to notify security and wait for a UN bomb unit to arrive. Delgado surely would have timed the bomb to go off shortly after Sloane accepted his award. Even with an evacuation already in progress, the building would still be full of people when the bomb exploded, flooding the United Nations with lethal doses of radiation. Hundreds of lives were at risk. He had to defuse the bomb sometime in the next few minutes.

Lurching from his chair, he ran to the stairway leading down to the floor of the General Assembly hall. "Merlin!" he exclaimed, contacting Marshall back at headquarters. "I'm going to try to defuse the bomb. You're going to have to talk me through it!"

"What?" Marshall sounded shocked. "Dix . . . Outrigger, there's no time. You've got to get out of there now!"

"Not an option!" Dixon replied. He knew he wouldn't be able to live with himself if he survived while scores of innocent civilians perished. He took the steps two at a time. "Work with me, Merlin!"

"Well, if you insist . . ." Marshall struggled audibly to keep his voice calm. "I still think this is a really bad idea, Outrigger, but, what the hell, I'm not going anywhere. . . ."

"Good man," Dixon said. He knew he could count on Marshall in a crunch. Reaching the bottom of the stairs, he charged through a fire door into the hall. With its multitude of seats now empty, only the wail of the fire alarm broke the eerie silence that had fallen over the hall. Dixon found himself deeply offended that anyone would dare to explode a bomb in a forum dedicated to world peace.

Sloane may deserve to die, he thought, *but that's no excuse for what Delgado has planned here. No revenge is worth the lives of so many innocent people!*

He found the forgotten trophy sitting on the podium where Sloane had left it. Ignoring the odious inscription, he removed a Swiss Army knife from his pocket and began unscrewing the silver plate on the base. "All right, Merlin. I'm opening it up now."

"Okay, Outrigger," Marshall said. "Raptor managed to pry the specs for the bomb out of Salvatore Genovese. I'm looking at them online right now. My guess is that the globe on top of the trophy contains the spherical casing holding the tritium and deuterium isotopes. You want to stay away from that. We're looking for the firing mechanism, which is probably hidden in the base somewhere." He was obviously thinking out loud. "That's how I'd do it, if I were inclined to build an enhanced radiation warhead into a bowling trophy, that is."

"Understood," Dixon acknowledged. He gently pried the plaque off the base, half-expecting the bomb to go off at any second. Would he even know if he failed, or would the neutron blast snuff out his life in less than a heartbeat? Sweat soaked through his suit as he raced against time. *Hang on, Diane,* he thought. *I may be joining you soon.* The faces of his children flashed through his mind. *Robin, Steven, I'm sorry we didn't have more time together. Forgive me for leaving you alone in the world.*

He recalled the last time he and Hayden Chase had made love. *Good-bye*, he wished her silently, experiencing a moment of profound regret. *Sorry we never had a chance to find out whether we had a future together.*

Beneath the plaque was a gray steel box with a backlit digital display. His gaze locked on the flickering red numerals.

00:00:30

Thirty seconds until detonation!

Pulling a camera phone from his pocket, he hastily sent Marshall a picture of the device.

"Okay," Marshall said, with a panicky squeak in his voice. "That looks like your standard GB-33A explosive ignition unit. You want to carefully disconnect that from the primary fusion apparatus in the sphere. If you lift it out of the base housing, you should see a couple of colored wires leading from the GB unit into the globe."

"Got that," Dixon said. Beads of perspiration dripped from his brow, and he impatiently wiped them away with the back of his head. "Here goes."

He dug his fingers into the seam between the ignition unit and obsidian base, then tugged on the firing mechanism.

It didn't budge.

He pulled harder, terrified of setting the unit off by mistake, but the results were the same. He didn't feel it give so much as a millimeter.

00:00:20

"Merlin!" he croaked hoarsely. "It's stuck. It won't come out!"

Marshall gasped. "It must be superglued in place!"

Dixon didn't like the sound of that. "Then how am I supposed to disconnect the wires?"

"You can't!" Desperation filled the other man's voice. "Dixon, it's impossible! Run for it!"

Dixon appreciated the sentiment, but it was already too late. He wouldn't even make it out of the Assembly Hall, let alone the building, before the bomb went off. He looked around frantically for something that might block the radiation blast, but realized that was an equally ridiculous option. The ionized neutrons released by the bomb were capable of penetrating the hulls of armored tanks. "Duck and cover" was not a viable strategy. He was doomed.

00:00:15

He tried to swallow, but his throat was too dry. His gaze was drawn to a pitcher of ice water resting atop the nearby podium. He wondered if he had time for one last sip, then froze as an even wilder idea popped into his brain.

What if . . . ?

There was no time to run the idea by Marshall, to see if it even made sense. *What do I have to lose?* he thought. Acting on instinct, he struck the ignition unit with his knife, cracking the clear plastic cover over the digital readout, then dropped the entire trophy into the pitcher. Cold water splashed against his wrists.

Sparks flew from the ruptured unit as the water invaded the delicate circuitry within. Dixon held his breath, wondering if he had hastened his end by a second or two. He prayed silently in anticipation of the world to come. Would Diane be there to greet him? He was ready to find out. . . .

But nothing happened.

The luminous red numerals lost their infernal glow, stuck at four seconds as the heavy trophy sank to the bottom of the clear crystal pitcher. Dixon let out a long, slow breath as he realized he was going to live.

He had done it. The bomb was defused. The United Nations was safe.

"Mission accomplished," he informed Marshall. Soaked with sweat, he slumped down onto the floor of the speaker's platform, beneath the gilded UN emblem. He felt emotionally and physically exhausted. "The bomb has been neutralized."

"What?" Marshall blurted out. "How?"

Dixon smiled at his friend's confusion. Marshall was likely to be embarrassed by Dixon's extremely low-tech solution to the crisis. *Sometimes the best way to put out a fire is with a plain old bucket of water.*

Too bad I had to save Arvin Sloane in the process.

CHAPTER 16

MEXICAN CONSULATE

"Thank God!"

A sigh of relief escaped Sydney's lips as Marshall informed her that Dixon had successfully defused the bomb at the UN. Disaster, it seemed, had been averted once again. *Now I just need to deal with Victor Delgado,* she realized. In theory, Manuel Rivera was keeping watch over the revenge-crazed ambassador down in the video-conferencing room. Too bad Rivera wasn't wearing a comm; otherwise, she could have informed him immediately that the missing neutron bomb was no longer a threat. Still, the communications center in the basement was only four floors down. She could tell him in person soon enough.

By now, Delgado must have realized that his scheme had gone awry. Sydney wondered how the ambassador was taking the news. *Not very well,* she guessed.

She glanced at the trophy she had removed from the safe, as well as the dossier on the Mexico City atrocity. Should she confiscate those as evidence? Probably, she realized, especially if the papers in the dossier linked Sloane to the attack on the church; Sloane's ability to run APO would be severely hampered if that information leaked out. *I can't believe I've been reduced to cleaning up Sloane's messes for him,* she thought in disgust as she stuffed the files into her handbag. His undeserved award felt heavy in her grip.

"Phoenix to headquarters," she addressed the team. "I'm about to take the target into custody. Prepare for an immediate extraction."

"Understood," Vaughn replied from across the street. Now that Catalina was no longer being blackmailed, he and Weiss had curtailed their round-the-clock surveillance of the ambassador's wife. Delgado was their only target now. "Ready when you are."

Technically, Sydney had no legal authority to apprehend the Mexican ambassador, especially on the grounds of his own consulate. APO seldom concerned itself with such niceties, however; it was one of the advantages of being officially off the books. And after what Victor Delgado had attempted to do, they could hardly leave him free to try again. Better that he disappear into APO's custody . . . indefinitely.

This is going to be tricky, she thought. The challenge would be to covertly remove Delgado from the premises without provoking the consulate's guards. *I just hope Rivera doesn't make a fuss.* Given Delgado's influence back in Mexico, Sydney was not willing to hand the corrupt ambassador over to CISEN or anyone else. *He's ours.*

Trophy in hand, she walked over to the open safe, intending to conceal any sign of her intrusion before she left the office. But before she could close the safe and remove the safecracking device, the office door swung open unexpectedly and Carlos Allende marched into the room. "What are you doing in here?" he demanded. His hostile gaze was instantly drawn to the emptied wall safe. He scowled beneath his mustache. "I knew you were not to be trusted!"

Damn! Sydney thought. The blackmailing security chief must have returned early from his meeting with the police commissioner. *Talk about bad timing!*

"Look," she said urgently, keeping her voice low to avoid attracting any attention from outside in the hall. "I know this looks bad, but you have to believe me, I have my reasons. Ambassador Delgado was behind a planned terrorist assault on the United Nations. Just close the door and let me explain."

Allende didn't care what she had to say. "I have no interest in the prevarications of American spies." He drew a Colt automatic from beneath his jacket and placed her squarely in the line of fire. "Stay where you are. You are now a prisoner of the Republic of Mexico."

This is not good, Sydney realized. Not only did she have more important things to do right now, but she could hardly count on the CIA to bail her out. APO was all about plausible deniability. *I'm on my own.*

Without taking his eyes away from her, Allende called for assistance. "Summon the guards!" he shouted to the secretary outside the door. *"Apuro!"*

"I'd think twice about that if I were you," Sydney warned him. "Unless you want me to tell the authorities, including Ambassador Delgado, about how you were blackmailing his wife, via your hired hands at Montezuma Protection Services."

The startled look in his eyes let Sydney know her threat had struck home. Stepping backward, he hurriedly closed and locked the door behind him to keep anyone from overhearing their incriminating conversation. "Who are you?" he asked angrily. His livid complexion highlighted the thin white scar on his cheek. "Who do you work for? How much do you know?"

"Enough," Sydney said, not wanting to feed the fire. Judging from his malignant expression, he was giving serious thought to silencing her once and for all. She decided to remind him that she wasn't working alone. "Who do you think threw a wrench into that meeting at the diner the other day? I hear your men aren't talking yet, but maybe if one of my associates dropped your name in the district attorney's ear?" She cradled Sloane's trophy in her arms. "Or perhaps you just let me walk away from here and I stay quiet?"

"No!" he said adamantly. "You're not going anywhere until you answer my questions." He glared at her down the barrel of his gun. "Who sent you here? What are you really after?"

Heavy knuckles rapped on the door. "Senor Allende?" a guard called to him. "Do you require assistance?"

Allende swore under his breath. Clearly, his staff members at the consulate were not privy to his blackmailing operation. He was in no hurry to expose the guard to Sydney's accusations. "Never mind!" he shouted back, turning toward the door. "It was a false alarm. You may return to your post!"

The instant his eyes were off her, Sydney sprang into action. With all her strength, she hurled the heavy trophy at Allende. The silver-plated award cracked against his head, and he dropped to his knees. *That's a better use for that damn trophy than the one the UN had in mind,* she thought.

She didn't give Allende a chance to cry out or recover. Lunging across the room, she whacked him across the back of his neck with an old-fashioned karate chop. He grunted once before falling limply on top of the handwoven Mexican rug.

Afraid that he might regain consciousness

before she could hustle Delgado out of the consulate and into APO's custody, she took a few moments to ensure he wouldn't bother her again. She gagged him with his tie, then found a pair of handcuffs inside his jacket. *Thank you, Senor Allende,* she thought. Cuffing his hands behind his back, she completed the job by removing the cord from the ambassador's infamous phone and using it to tie Allende's ankles together, before dragging him back behind the desk where he could not be seen. When she was done, she felt confident that the downed security chief would not be going anywhere soon.

Tucking Allende's Colt into the waistband of her skirt and pulling her tweed jacket down over its grip, she mussed her hair and smeared her lipstick before heading for the door. *What the heck,* she thought, *I might as well use this trick again. Iris's reputation is already shot.*

She stepped outside into the hall and quickly drew the door shut behind her. "Senor Allende said it was okay for me to go," she said to whoever might be listening. Smirks and arched eyebrows greeted her disheveled appearance; Sydney felt as though she had single-handedly sullied the good name of female American grad students throughout the entire Mexican Consulate. "He's taking care of everything for me."

"I'll bet," someone muttered by the Xerox machine.

Ignoring the whispers and muffled laughter, she hurried to the stairwell and rushed down to the basement, where she found Rivera standing outside the closed door of the video-conferencing room. The lit red bulb above the door indicated that Ambassador Delgado was still inside, even though the award ceremony had been interrupted by the bomb scare. She imagined him sitting before the screen, on which he had expected to witness Arvin Sloane's grisly demise, realizing that his carefully crafted assassination plot had amounted to nothing. *Does he know that the jig is up?* she wondered. *Is he expecting someone to come for him?*

She hoped he would surrender without a fight.

"Iris!" Rivera said as she approached. He looked around to make sure they were alone. "Did you find anything?"

Sydney quickly filled him in on everything that had happened since she had discovered the trophy in Delgado's safe, leaving out only the fact that she and her team were affiliated with Arvin Sloane. It was enough to tell him that Sloane was the target, and that the neutron bomb had been neutralized before it went off.

"Thank heaven!" he said in a hushed tone. "I can't believe that Delgado would go so far as to bomb the UN, just to kill one man. He must be insane!"

You weren't there in Mexico City, she thought. What had happened at that church was enough to drive any man over the edge. She gestured toward the door. "What's going on with him?"

"I thought I heard him cry out once, but since then . . . silence." He shrugged his shoulders. "I didn't want to disturb him as long as you were busy in his office."

"Good call." She drew Allende's gun from beneath her jacket. "See if you can persuade him to come out of there."

Rivera eyed her gun suspiciously. "What do you have in mind?"

"Listen to me, Manuel . . . or whatever your real name is." Sydney wasn't going to mince words. "I'm taking Delgado and I don't want any arguments about it."

He frowned. "This is a Mexican matter. We have jurisdiction here."

"Not when your ambassador is responsible for an attempted terrorist attack in the heart of New York City. In case you haven't heard, we frown on that these days." In a pinch, she figured the Colt gave her the deciding vote, but she was hoping it wouldn't come to that. "Besides, you and I both know that his connections back in Mexico aren't going to do him an ounce of good where we're going to put him." She looked him squarely in the eyes. "Leave him to us. I promise he'll get what's coming to him."

"Well, when you put it that way . . ." Rivera sounded less than thrilled by the plan, but he seemed to be coming around. "We'll need some sort of cover story. To avoid a scandal, not to mention an embarrassing international incident."

"Of course." She could see that the Mexican government wouldn't want it known that one of their representatives nearly irradiated the United Nations. All the more reason why Delgado should simply disappear into APO custody. "You can say that he's gone into hiding, in response to death threats from the drug traffickers."

It struck her that, in the end, the ambassador's upcoming presentation to the UN Commission on Narcotic Drugs had nothing to do with the assassination plot involving the Genovese brothers. *We were looking in the wrong direction the whole time.*

Rivera nodded. "Yes, that could work, I suppose."

"In any event, I'm sure you can come up with something," she said curtly. "But we don't have time to debate this all morning. Call him."

Giving in, the Mexican agent knocked on the door of the video-conferencing room. "Mr. Ambassador? It's me, Manuel. I need to speak with you immediately."

"Go away!" a hysterical voice shouted from behind the door. Sydney barely recognized the source as Victor Delgado. "Leave me alone!"

She motioned to Rivera to try again.

"Ambassador Delgado!" he called again, raising his voice. He tried the doorknob, but it was locked from the inside. "Forgive me for disturbing you, but this just can't wait. Please open the door!"

This time only silence answered the deputy's entreaties.

Sydney didn't like the way this was going. Delgado sounded like he was unraveling fast. *How far gone is he?* she worried. *Enough to harm himself?* She remembered Niccolo Genovese committing suicide in front of her very eyes, and she resolved not to let that happen again. Especially for Mercedes's sake; the teen was going to have a rough enough time over the next few weeks without her stepfather killing himself as well.

"We need to get in there," she said. "Before he does something drastic."

Rivera nodded in agreement. "Permit me," he volunteered. Stepping back to get a running start, he rammed his shoulder into the door. A resounding thud echoed across the basement, but the door remained standing. "Just a few more blows," he promised, backing up to try again. "I'm sure I felt it wobble a bit."

Sydney took his word for it. She was tempted to shoot the lock off, but she knew that the sound of a gunshot would immediately draw a small army of guards to the scene. *Not my ideal scenario,* she thought, still hoping to extract Delgado from the consulate without any messy confrontations with the security forces upstairs. She tapped her foot restlessly on the floor. *This is taking too long. . . .*

She was about to add her muscle to Rivera's

when the CISEN agent slammed into the door for the third time, which proved to be the charm. The lock gave way and the door swung open into the dimly lit chamber beyond. Rivera's momentum carried him halfway through the doorway. "Mr. Ambassador?" he asked tentatively.

"Wait!" Sydney called out as the unarmed deputy charged inside. He got as far as the outer edge of the door when something smashed against the back of his skull. Sydney heard an ugly crack and watched in dismay as Rivera collapsed face-first onto the floor of the chamber. "Manuel!"

She realized instantly that Delgado had been lying in wait just behind the door. She lunged forward and kicked the door with all her might, sending it rebounding back against the man on the other side. A gasp of pain and the sound of the solid oak connecting with a soft human body indicated that her kick had achieved the desired effect. Brandishing the Colt, she leaped over Rivera's prone body and spun around to face the disgraced ambassador. "Don't move! I'll shoot if I have to!"

The only light in the room came from the wall-size TV screen behind her. Sydney suspected that the monitor was still displaying the now-empty

General Assembly Hall, but she didn't risk looking over her shoulder to find out. As her eyes adjusted to the gloom, she spotted Victor Delgado, trapped between the door and the wall behind it. His right hand still clutched the crystal paperweight he must have used to clobber Rivera.

"Iris?" he blurted out in confusion.

Nice to know my alias fooled somebody, she thought.

"Drop it!"

The paperweight hit the carpet with a thud, and she knelt to check on Rivera. His pulse and breathing were steady, so she guessed that he was just out cold. Maybe a concussion at worst. Convinced that the agent's injury was not life-threatening, she rose to her feet, keeping her gun trained on Delgado. "Now step out where I can see you!"

The man who emerged from behind the door bore little resemblance to the charming, charismatic diplomat Sydney remembered. His silver hair was in disarray, and raw fury blazed in his eyes. "What is the meaning of this?" he protested. "You pull a gun on me in my own home?"

"It's over," she told him bluntly, not bothering

to waste time with explanations. "We know all about the bomb . . . and what you intended to do with it."

Understanding dawned in the ambassador's eyes. "You! This is your fault! You're the one who spared that monster's life!" He glared at her with contempt. "You're one of Sloane's minions, aren't you? I should have guessed as much!" His voice grew even more virulent as his scornful words hit a little too close to home. *A lucky guess,* she wondered, *or does he just see Sloane behind every conspiracy against him?* "Do you know what that fiend did to my homeland, to my people? He launched an unprovoked attack on my country . . . and on a house of God, no less!"

I know, Sydney thought. *I was there.* She recalled that Delgado had been raised by nuns in Mexico City. Was that another reason why the massacre at the church had so unhinged him?

"I lost many dear friends in that attack," he ranted. "Then to learn, years later, that the United Nations intended to honor the very man responsible for the atrocity . . . !" He clenched his fists. "Such an abomination demanded retribution!"

She knew how he felt. "But why bomb the

entire Assembly building?" she asked. "Why kill all those innocent people too?"

"Innocent?" He spat out the word. "When they conspire to pay tribute to a man like Arvin Sloane?" He glared at her. "If the United Nations wants to reward a monster like Sloane, then let them feel the pain his victims felt!"

There was no point in arguing with Delgado any further. "I'm sorry, but I'm afraid you have to come with me." She put the automatic weapon in the pocket of her jacket "You're going to walk through that door, up the stairs, and out the front door of the consulate, without a word to the guards. Is that clear?"

"You can't arrest me!" he objected. "This is Mexican soil . . . I have diplomatic immunity."

"You've mistaken me for someone who cares." Cupping a hand over her ear, Sydney contacted Vaughn and Weiss. "I have the target. Meet me in front of the consulate."

"The car is out front and running," Vaughn told her. "We're just waiting on you and your traveling companion."

"Great," she said. If all went well, this mission was minutes away from being over. She made a mental note to call the consulate from the car to let them know that Rivera needed medical attention. "All right." She let the barrel of the Colt bulge through the fabric of her jacket, as a reminder to Delgado that she could shoot him at any time if he failed to cooperate. "Out the door."

"This is an outrage!" he blustered. "A violation of international law!"

"And killing everyone at the UN isn't?" She took a second to pat the ambassador's unruly hair into place, so that he looked less disheveled and more under control. Then she got behind Delgado and prodded him toward the door. "Remember, not a word to the guards."

As he stepped through the doorway, however, Sydney heard footsteps running toward them. "Iris? Are you down here?" an excited voice chirped out in the hall. "Guess what? I found this really great book on Krav Maga at the library!"

Mercedes! No! Sydney thought in alarm. Before she could stop him, Delgado grabbed the girl by her collar and spun her around, turning his stepdaughter into a human shield. "Stand back!" he warned Sydney savagely. "Or I'll break her neck!"

"What's going on?" Fear and confusion washed over Mercedes's face. "Let go of me!"

"Quiet, you brat!" Delgado hissed in her ear. He had one arm around her waist and an elbow at her throat. He backed away from Sydney, dragging Mercedes with him. He nodded at Sydney. "Drop that gun!"

"All right!" she said quickly, not wanting to provoke the desperate ambassador. Mercedes's safety was all that mattered now. She slowly removed the Colt from her pocket and laid it down on the carpet by her feet. "Stay calm!" she urged him. "You don't want to hurt her."

Delgado laughed bitterly. "That's what you think." He tightened his grip around the girl's throat and Mercedes let out a plaintive squeak. Her frightened eyes widened further as she spotted Rivera's motionless body lying on the carpet. "Kick the gun away!"

Sydney did as he instructed, then tried to reason with him. "Think about what you're doing, Victor. She's your stepdaughter, for God's sake."

"A burden and an embarrassment, you mean!" His voice held not a trace of warmth or affection. "I would have already rid myself of her if you hadn't interfered in the subway!" He shook his head ruefully. "That alone should have tipped me off that you were not who you seemed. . . ."

"You were behind the kidnapping?" Oddly enough, Sydney was surprised to find herself caught off guard by this revelation. *I should have seen that coming.* Anyone willing to vaporize countless UN delegates and sightseers was obviously capable of plotting a routine kidnapping.

"Of course!" he boasted. "What better way to get back at my cheating whore of a wife, and pry open her private accounts?" A sneer twisted his lips as he spoke of Catalina. "Neutron bombs cost money, you know, and an abduction seemed more profitable than shipping the little demon off to boarding school."

Tears fell from Mercedes's eyes as she was forced to listen to her stepfather's cruel remarks. *What hurt more,* Sydney wondered, *the verbal attacks on her or on her mother?*

Or maybe she was just fearing for her life.

Anger flared in Sydney's heart. "Let me guess. You were behind the blackmail, too?" Obviously, the ambassador knew all about his wife's infidelities. "Allende was working for you?"

"Naturally," he taunted her. "It seems you didn't know as much as you thought you did." He hauled his hostage farther down the corridor, away from Sydney. "Mercedes and I are going for a little walk now. Don't try to follow me if you care at all about your so-called student. As far as I'm concerned, her life isn't worth a speck. We would have all been better off if she was never born!"

Mercedes had heard enough. *"Hijo de puta!"*

Throwing her head back, she bashed her skull into Delgados's face. Then, just as Sydney had taught her, she turned her head and yanked down on her stepfather's forearm with both hands, before sliding back under his right shoulder. Dazed and disoriented, he toppled forward—just in time to feel Mercedes's knee jab into his stomach. He gasped in pain, losing his grip on her waist. Blood streamed from his nose as the girl pulled herself clear of him completely.

"Iris!"

The frightened girl ran forward into Sydney's arms. The female agent felt a rush of emotion as she realized Mercedes was safe. *Thank goodness she paid attention in those training sessions!*

Behind her, Delgado scrambled to his feet and

made a break for it. Sydney had no idea where the would-be terrorist thought he was going, and she doubted that Delgado knew either. Diplomatic immunity notwithstanding, he had to know that the U.S. government was never going to let him get away with smuggling a neutron bomb into the country. Foreign nationals had been shipped off to Guantanamo Bay for less.

She gently disengaged herself from Mercedes's embrace. "I have to go after him, you realize that?" The girl nodded and wiped the tears from her eyes. Sydney examined her face for signs of trauma. "Are you going to be okay?"

"Don't worry about me." She looked over at Rivera, who was still dead to the world. She gulped at the sight of the injured deputy. "What about him?"

"Stay here for one minute, then go find help," Sydney instructed her. "He should be okay, though." She heard Delgado's frantic footsteps on the stairs and realized that she couldn't wait any longer. Recovering her gun, she turned to leave Mercedes. "And, by the way, I'm proud of you."

Mercedes beamed back at her.

With that, Sydney took off after Delgado. Colt in hand, she ran up the steps, startling clerks and assistants who happened to be taking the stairs at the time. "Out of the way!" she shouted, which proved unnecessary since people instinctively scrambled away from her at the sight of the gun, throwing themselves against the walls of the stairwell or retreating back to the nearest floor. "I'm with CISEN!"

Rivera would have some explaining to do afterward, but that wasn't her problem. She only wished she'd had time to search him for a badge.

Younger and in better shape than Delgado, she was rapidly gaining on the fleeing ambassador as he ascended the stairs. At first, she was surprised that he didn't run for the exit on the first floor, then she remembered that Delgado had heard her arranging the extraction with Vaughn. He knew she had confederates waiting out front.

"Bad news," she notified her team as she ran. Years of strenuous physical conditioning allowed her to speak clearly into the comm even while sprinting up the steps. "The target is on the run. I'm in pursuit."

"We read you, Phoenix," Vaughn responded, his voice tense. She imagined him and Weiss exchanging a worried look in the front seat of the

Subaru. "Do you require reinforcements?"

"Negative, Shotgun." The last thing Hayden Chase wanted was black ops agents charging into a foreign consulate in broad daylight. "Stand by."

Floor after floor, she chased Delgado through the brownstone. Soon she could hear his labored breathing and glimpse his ankles on the steps above her. "Give it up, Delgado!" she shouted. "You've got nowhere to run!"

Despite everything he'd done, including the blackmail and attempted kidnapping, she still felt sorry for the man. Lord knows he had a legitimate reason to want Sloane dead, even if that obsession had endangered far too many innocent people to be overlooked. *He crossed the line,* she thought, *but I don't want to have to kill him.*

A door opened above her and a cold wind invaded the stairwell. *He's run out onto the roof,* she realized. The door slammed shut loudly, a second before Sydney reached the landing at the top of the stairs. She kicked the door open again and advanced cautiously, not wanting to get ambushed like Rivera had. She held the automatic weapon in front of her with both hands as she stepped out from behind the door.

Smoke rose from a brick chimney nearby, while whirring turbine vents helped circulate the air in the floors below. A sooty white satellite dish rested on the floor not far from the stairwell. Sydney recalled running across this very rooftop the night of the blackout. *At least I didn't have to scale the side of the building this time.*

She spotted Delgado standing several yards away. Exhausted from the climb, the fifty-something ambassador was gasping for breath. Bent over, resting his hands on his knees, he was huffing and puffing so hard that Sydney was worried that he'd have a heart attack before she could bring him in.

"It's the end of the line, Victor," she announced. The frigid air cooled the sweat beneath her clothes and her breath misted before her lips. "Make it easy on yourself and surrender."

He straightened up at the sound of her voice. His eyes darted toward the fire escape at the rear of the building that led down to the enclosed courtyard behind the brownstone. Sydney moved to block off that escape route.

"Go ahead and shoot. I've lost everything." Spite and self-pity dripped from his voice. "What else do I have to live for?"

"Who knows?" Sydney said. "If you cooperate, you may live long enough to see Arvin Sloane get his just deserts someday." She still expected Sloane to show his true colors sometime in the future, probably at the worst possible moment. "That day will come, trust me."

"You expect me to believe that? Don't insult my intelligence!" He stared at her incredulously, as though she were the insane one. Sydney couldn't help wondering how much he knew about Sloane's current activities and status. "I'd rather die than fall into the hands of that devil!"

Without warning, he dashed toward the chimney. Sydney's finger hesitated on the trigger, and he ducked behind the protective brick structure. *Damn!* she thought. *He's not making this easy.*

She considered the Midtown roofscape surrounding them, evaluating Delgado's options. Immediately to the west, a twenty-foot skyscraper towered above the brownstone, so that a straight vertical plane ruled out any hope of escape in that direction. To the east was a five-story office building, one floor shorter than the consulate building. A large wooden water tank sat on stilts atop the building's level roof.

That's the way I'd go.

"You're just delaying the inevitable!" she shouted as she began to circle around the chimney, hoping to get between Delgado and the smaller building next door. She heard loud voices and pounding footsteps coming from the stairs. *Allende's guards,* she guessed. *They're responding to the commotion.* "You can't get away!"

"We'll see about that, *puta*!" Realizing what she was up to, he broke from cover and raced toward the ledge overlooking the office building. Sydney took aim with her gun, but the corner of the chimney briefly obstructed her shot. Not that she really wanted to fire. *He's twice my age,* she thought. *I should be able to bring him down without shooting him in the back.*

Delgado took off at a run and leaped from the roof onto the next building, dropping out of Sydney's line of sight. She rushed to the ledge and peered down at the escaping diplomat. He must have landed badly, because he was limping noticeably as he ran toward one of the stout wooden pillars supporting the water tank. He glanced back fearfully over his shoulder, perhaps hoping that "Iris" would not risk the jump herself.

Fat chance, Sydney thought. She sprang from the ledge, landing nimbly on the tar roof one story below. Her well-toned legs absorbed the impact, and she was running toward the looming water tower within seconds of hitting the ground. *So much for territorial issues,* she mused. *We're not on Mexican soil anymore.*

Sydney heard a door slam open above her and spun around to see a crowd of security guards pour out onto the roof of the consulate. She heard them shouting in confusion. With luck, she'd have a few seconds before they realized where she and Delgado had gone.

"Madre de Dios!" the ambassador exclaimed as he saw her coming. He turned and bolted, dragging his injured leg behind him. "Leave me alone, you bitch!"

"Sorry, Victor!" she called after him. "Not going to happen!"

She looked ahead of them. Beyond the roof of the office building, a narrow alley separated the structure from the multistory apartment complex directly to the east. A series of tiered setbacks commenced on the fifth floor, opposite the roof of the office building, so that the higher floors resembled vast glass-and-steel steps ascending toward the sky. Delgado reached the end of the roof and paused at the edge of the precipice. He seemed to be weighing his chances of reaching the rooftop across the way.

"No!" Sydney yelled in alarm. If she shot him now, he would surely tumble over the edge. She slowed to a halt, for fear of spurring him to leap to his death. "Don't do it, Victor!"

He looked back at her over his shoulder. His weathered face held a trace of his former dignity. "Tell Sloane I'll see him in hell."

To her horror, he backed up and hurled himself into the empty air dividing the two buildings. His hands reached out for the outer edge of the setback in front of him, but it was farther away than it looked; even without a bad leg, he probably would not have made it. Gravity seized him and his fingers fell short of their target by several inches. A high-pitched shriek escaped his lips as he plummeted out of sight. A half second later Sydney heard his body crash against the pavement below.

Oh my God! She hurried to the edge of the roof, even though she knew it was already too late. Peering over the ledge, she saw the ambassador's lifeless body sprawled on the litter-strewn floor of the alley, only a few feet away from a rusty steel Dumpster. A dark red puddle spread out from beneath his fractured skull.

Sydney shook her head sadly. This was not how she had wanted to finish this mission. In the end, despite his own crimes, Victor Delgado had become just another victim of Arvin Sloane's murderous past.

It didn't feel like much of a victory.

EPILOGUE

SOUTH AMERICAN GALLERY
METROPOLITAN MUSEUM OF ART
MANHATTAN

The rooms were hushed as Sydney strolled through the first-floor gallery at the Met. Glass display cases held an impressive collection of Pre-Columbian artifacts from South and Central America. Gold, silver, and jade jewelry gleamed within the cases, along with finely crafted pottery and statues. Brightly colored textiles were mounted on the neutral tan walls. The awed expressions on the faces of the museum patrons testified to the splendor of the collection, which boasted the most comprehensive display of American gold objects in the world. As it was only

11 A.M. on a Wednesday, the gallery was sparsely populated, so Sydney had no trouble locating the person she had come to meet.

Mercedes was seated on a low stone bench, admiring a seventh-century Peruvian tunic. The red-and-yellow geometric pattern on the dyed cotton garment remained vibrant even after fourteen centuries. The fluorescent purple streaks in the girl's hair seemed to fit right in.

"Hi there, stranger," Sydney said as she quietly sat down beside Mercedes. "Getting some fashion tips?"

"Iris!" The teenager's eyes lit up as she greeted Sydney, and she threw her arms around her former teacher. The girl's outburst provoked a few disapproving glares from other museum-goers, and she sheepishly lowered her voice. "You came!"

Sydney hugged her back. "Was there any doubt? You didn't think I was going to let my favorite pupil flee the country without saying goodbye first, did you?" She glanced around at the elegant gallery. "I'm just glad I finally got you here. It would have been a shame if you'd left New York without ever seeing the Met."

"Yeah, there's some cool stuff here," Mercedes

conceded, letting go of the other woman. Sydney knew that, by teenage standards, that constituted a ringing endorsement. "I've got to admit, though, I skipped the subway this time and splurged on a cab instead."

"I don't blame you!" Sydney said. Memories of that unusually eventful field trip flashed through her brain. Her voice took on a more serious tone, and she looked into the girl's face with concern. "So, how are you doing these days? Really?"

Three weeks had passed since Victor Delgado had fallen to his death. Officially, the story was that the ambassador had died in a freak accident, completely unrelated to the bomb scare at the General Assembly building. So far the press and the public seemed to be accepting the cover story, perhaps because the true story—that a respected foreign ambassador had smuggled a neutron bomb into the United Nations—was too outlandish to be believed. To Sydney's relief, the cover-up had also spared Mercedes and her mother from any sort of public scandal. *That's something, at least,* she thought.

"I'm okay, I guess," Mercedes answered with a shrug. "The new ambassador is due at the end of the week, so the plan is for us to move out and get settled back in Mexico before then." She didn't sound at all unhappy to be leaving the New York consulate behind. "My mom's a mess, of course, but Ramon is helping her through it." She rolled her eyes at the thought. "I suppose he's an improvement over my evil stepdad."

Just be thankful you never saw the videotape, Sydney thought. She glanced across the gallery to where the muscular bodyguard was pretending to be interested in a solid gold Mayan fertility idol. She had spotted Ramon within seconds of entering the gallery, but she could hardly blame him and Catalina for wanting to keep a close eye on Mercedes. After all that had happened, the bodyguard's presence was a reasonable precaution, even though Sydney judged that the teenager was in little danger now that Delgado was dead and Carlos Allende had been deported to Mexico.

According to Manuel Rivera, who had taken part in Allende's lengthy interrogations after recovering from his head injury, the general consensus among the investigators was that the former security chief had not been privy to Delgado's plans regarding the neutron bomb. He may have supervised the kidnapping and blackmail schemes directed at Catalina, but apparently Victor Delgado had kept his most ambitious—and nightmarish—plan to himself. In the end, as a concession to Mexican sovereignty, the U.S. had been content to simply kick the corrupt security chief out of the country. Rivera had assured Sydney, however, that CISEN would be keeping a close eye on Allende from now on. *If I were him,* she thought, *I'd watch my step.*

For a moment she and Ramon made eye contact. Although his stolid face barely moved, he gave her a respectful nod, a greeting from one professional to another. Sydney hoped that he and the newly widowed Catalina would be good for each other in the long run, even though they were currently keeping their relationship discreetly low profile. As Sydney contemplated the looming bodyguard, she was almost disappointed that they had never actually come to blows, if only to find out who would come out on top.

I still think I could take him.

"Anyway, I'm looking forward to seeing my friends again," Mercedes continued. Sydney turned her attention back to her former student. "And my mom's promising to spend more time with me once we're settled in back home." She sighed theatrically. "I haven't decided if that's a good thing or not."

Be grateful, Sydney advised her silently. *At least your mom never worked for the KGB.* She decided to give Catalina the benefit of the doubt; maybe she really was going to be a more attentive mother from now on. "That's great! I'm glad that everything seems to be coming together for you."

"Thanks, Iris!" Mercedes paused and gave Sydney a quizzical look. "So, I'm guessing your name isn't really Iris."

"Not really," she admitted. "If you want, though, I can set up an e-mail account where you can write me care of that name."

"That would be terrific!" Mercedes said, gazing at Sydney with pure admiration. She leaned forward and whispered so that no one else could hear. "This is all so cool. When I grow up, I want to be a kick-ass secret agent just like you."

Sydney winced at the thought. Although she knew that the work she did was essential to the world's safety, she also knew the toll that years of lies, betrayal, and violence had taken on her heart; that wasn't something she wished on the eager young teen. "Not so fast," she said sincerely. "Trust me, you don't want to limit your options by trying to emulate someone else. I spent years trying to be the woman I thought my mother was, and . . . well, that didn't really work out." She looked intently into Mercedes's eyes. "You need to find your own passion, your own calling."

"Even though I have no idea what that is?" Mercedes asked.

"You will," Sydney promised. "Someday."

"Okay," Mercedes said thoughtfully. "I won't rush into anything." If nothing else, the depth of Sydney's feeling seemed to have gotten through to the younger woman. "That reminds me. I have something for you."

She reached beneath the bench and produced a tinted plastic folder containing several pages of paper. "What's this?" Sydney asked as Mercedes passed the folder over to her. She flipped open the cover to read the first page:

Alone in the Woods:
"The Road Not Taken" vs. *The Divine Comedy*
by Mercedes Torres

"Five thousand words on Robert Frost and Dante," the girl explained, blushing slightly. "And not downloaded from the Internet, I promise."

Sydney felt a lump in her throat. "You didn't have to do this."

"Sure I did." She beamed at Sydney. "I don't care if it was just an act, you're still the best teacher I ever had."

"I wasn't faking all of it," Sydney insisted, moved by the girl's unsolicited testimonial. *How about that? Maybe all that training to be a teacher wasn't a totally wasted effort.* She couldn't see herself going back to grad school anytime soon—APO was her top priority now—but perhaps, when she got back to Los Angeles, she could volunteer to tutor struggling students in her spare time. At the moment she couldn't think of anything more rewarding.

Who knows? she thought. *Maybe there's a little Laura Bristow in me after all.*

ABOUT THE AUTHOR

Greg Cox is the *New York Times* bestselling author of numerous books, including the first APO novel, *Two of a Kind?* He also wrote the official movie novelizations of *Daredevil* and *Underworld*, as well as books and short stories based on such popular series as Batman, Buffy the Vampire Slayer, Fantastic Four, Farscape, Iron Man, Roswell, Spider-Man, Star Trek, Underworld, X-Men, and Xena: Warrior Princess.

He lives in Oxford, Pennsylvania.